# HIGH PROFILE

# HIGH PROFILE

ROBERT B. PARKER

G. P. PUTNAM'S SONS

*New York*

G. P. PUTNAM'S SONS
*Publishers Since 1838*
Published by the Penguin Group
Penguin Group (USA) Inc., 375 Hudson Street, New York, New York 10014, USA •
Penguin Group (Canada), 90 Eglinton Avenue East, Suite 700, Toronto, Ontario
M4P 2Y3, Canada (a division of Pearson Penguin Canada Inc.) • Penguin Books Ltd,
80 Strand, London WC2R 0RL, England • Penguin Ireland, 25 St Stephen's Green, Dublin 2,
Ireland (a division of Penguin Books Ltd) • Penguin Group (Australia), 250 Camberwell
Road, Camberwell, Victoria 3124, Australia (a division of Pearson Australia Group
Pty Ltd) • Penguin Books India Pvt Ltd, 11 Community Centre, Panchsheel Park, New
Delhi–110 017, India • Penguin Group (NZ), 67 Apollo Drive, Mairangi Bay, Auckland
1311, New Zealand (a division of Pearson New Zealand Ltd) • Penguin Books (South
Africa) (Pty) Ltd, 24 Sturdee Avenue, Rosebank, Johannesburg 2196, South Africa

Penguin Books Ltd, Registered Offices:
80 Strand, London WC2R 0RL, England

Library of Congress Cataloging-in-Publication Data

Parker, Robert B.
High profile / Robert B. Parker.
p.    cm.
ISBN 978-0-399-15404-1
Stone, Jesse (Fictitious character)—Fiction.    2. Police—Massachusetts—Fiction.
3. Police chiefs—Fiction.    4. Massachusetts—Fiction.    I. Title.
PS3566.A686H54    2007                2006037328
813'.54—dc22

Printed in the United States of America
1   3   5   7   9   10   8   6   4   2

This book is printed on acid-free paper. ∞

BOOK DESIGN BY AMANDA DEWEY

*For Joan,* whom the eyes of mortals
have no right to see

# HIGH
# PROFILE

Each spring surprised Jesse. In the years since he'd come to Paradise he never remembered, from year to year, how pretty spring was in the Northeast. He stood now among the opening flowers and the new leaves, looking at a dead man, hanging by his neck from the limb of a tree in the park, on Indian Hill, overlooking the harbor.

Peter Perkins was taking pictures. Suitcase Simpson was running crime-scene tape and shooing away onlookers. Molly Crane sat in a squad car, talking with a woman in jogging clothes. Molly was writing in her notebook.

"Doesn't look like his neck is broken," Jesse said.

Perkins nodded.

"Hands are free," Jesse said.

Perkins nodded.

"Nothing to jump off of," Jesse said. "Unless he went up in the tree and jumped from the limb."

Perkins nodded.

"Open his coat," Peter Perkins said.

Jesse opened the raincoat. An argyle sweater beneath the coat was dark and stiff with dried blood.

"There goes the suicide theory," Jesse said.

"ME will tell us," Perkins said, "but my guess is he was dead before he got hung."

Jesse walked around the area, looking at the ground. At one point he squatted on his heels and looked at the grass.

"They had already shot him," Jesse said. "And dragged him over . . ."

"Sometimes I forget you grew up out west," Perkins said.

Jesse grinned and walked toward the tree, still looking down.

"And looped the rope around his neck . . ."

Jesse looked up at the corpse.

"Tossed the rope over the tree limb, hauled him up, and tied the rope around the trunk."

"Good-sized guy," Perkins said.

"About two hundred?" Jesse said.

Perkins looked appraisingly at the corpse and nodded.

"Dead weight," Perkins said.

"So to speak," Jesse said.

"Maybe more than one person involved," Perkins said.

Jesse nodded.

"ID?" Jesse said.

"None," Perkins said. "No wallet, nothing."

Another Paradise police car pulled up with its blue light revolving, and Arthur Angstrom got out.

"Anyone minding the store?" Jesse said.

Angstrom was looking at the hanging corpse.

"Maguire," Angstrom said. "Suicide?"

"I wish," Jesse said.

The blue light on Angstrom's cruiser stayed on.

"Murder?" Angstrom said.

"Peter Perkins will fill you in," Jesse said. "After you shut off your light."

Angstrom glanced back at the cruiser, and looked at Jesse for a moment as if he were going to argue. Jesse looked back at him, and Angstrom turned and shut off his light.

"Car keys?" Jesse said.

"Nope."

"So how'd he get here?"

"Walked?" Perkins said.

Angstrom joined them.

"Or came with the killers," Jesse said.

"Or met them here," Perkins said, "and one of them drove his car away after he was hanging."

"Or took a cab," Jesse said.

"I can check that out," Angstrom said.

Jesse looked at his watch.

"Eight thirty," he said. "Town cab should be open now."

"I'll call them," Arthur said. "I know the dispatcher."

"Arthur, you're the cops, you don't have to know the dispatcher."

"Sure," Angstrom said, "of course."

He walked to his car. Jesse watched him go.

"Arthur ain't never quite got used to being a cop," Peter Perkins said.

"Arthur hasn't gotten fully used to being Arthur," Jesse said.

Jesse slid into the backseat of the cruiser, where Molly was talking to the young woman.

"This is Kate Mahoney," Molly said. "She found the body."

"I'm Jesse Stone," he said.

"The police chief," the woman said.

"Yes," Jesse said. "How are you?"

The woman nodded. She was holding a middle-aged beagle in her lap.

"I'm okay," she said.

Jesse looked at Molly. Molly nodded. Yes, she was okay. Jesse scratched the beagle behind an ear.

"Tell me what you saw," Jesse said.

"I just told her," the woman said.

She was probably thirty, brown hair tucked up under a baseball cap. Blue sweatpants, white T-shirt, elaborate running shoes. Jesse nodded.

"I know," he said. "Police bureaucracy. You were out running?"

"Yes, I run every morning before I have breakfast."

"Good for you," Jesse said. "You usually run up here?"

"Yes. I like the hill."

"So you came up here this morning as usual . . ." Jesse said.

"And I saw him. . . ." She closed her eyes for a moment. "Hanging there."

Jesse was quiet. The woman shook her head briefly, and opened her eyes.

"See anybody else?"

"No, just . . ."

She made a sort of rolling gesture with her right hand. The beagle watched the movement with his ears pricked slightly.

"Just the man on the tree?" Jesse said.

"Yes."

"You know who he is?" Jesse said.

"No. I didn't really look. When I saw him, I ran off and called nine-one-one on my cell phone."

"And here we are," Jesse said.

"I don't want to look at him," the woman said.

"You don't have to," Jesse said. "Is there anything else you can tell us that will help us figure out who did this?"

" 'Did this'? It's not suicide?"

"No," Jesse said.

"You mean somebody murdered him?"

"Yes," Jesse said.

"Omigod," she said. "I don't want any trouble."

"You just discovered the body. You won't have any trouble."

"Will I have to testify?"

"Not up to me," Jesse said. "But you don't have much to testify about that Molly or I couldn't testify about."

"I don't want any trouble."

"You'll be fine," Jesse said. "I promise."

The woman hugged her dog and pressed her face against the top of his head.

"You'll both be fine," Jesse said. "Officer Crane will drive you home."

The woman nodded with her cheek pressed against the dog's head. The dog looked uneasy. Jesse gave her one of his cards.

"You think of anything," Jesse said, "or anything bothers you, call me. Or Officer Crane."

The woman nodded. Jesse scratched the beagle under the chin and got out of the car.

J esse was in the squad room with Molly Crane, Suitcase
Simpson, and Peter Perkins. They were drinking coffee.

"State lab has him," Peter Perkins said. "They'll fingerprint the body and run the prints. They haven't autopsied
him yet, but I'll bet they find he died of gunshot. I didn't
see any exit wounds, so I'm betting they find the slugs in
there when they open him up."

"Had to have happened last night," Suitcase said. "I mean,
people are in that park all the time. He couldn't have hung
there long without being spotted."

Jesse nodded and glanced at Peter Perkins.

"I haven't seen all that many dead bodies," Perkins said. "And very few who were hanged from a tree. But this guy looks like he's been dead longer than that."

Jesse nodded.

"And . . ." Peter Perkins glanced at Molly.

"And he smells," Molly said. "I noticed it, too."

Jesse nodded.

"And there was no blood except on him. He got shot and hanged, he'd have bled out and there'd be blood on the ground," Suitcase said.

"So," Jesse said. "He was shot somewhere else and kept awhile before they brought him up to the hill and hanged him."

"You think it's more than one?" Molly said.

"A two-hundred-pound corpse is hard for one person to manhandle around and hoist over a limb," Jesse said.

"But not impossible," Molly said.

"No," Jesse said.

They all sat quietly.

"Anyone reported missing?" Jesse said.

"No," Molly said.

"Anyone else know anything?"

"Nobody I talked with," Suitcase said.

Molly Crane and Peter Perkins both shook their heads.

"Even if you knew the guy," Simpson said, "be kind of hard to recognize him now."

"Anyone want to speculate why you'd shoot some guy," Jesse said, "hold his body until it started to ripen, and then hang it on a tree?"

"Symbolic," Molly said. "It must have some sort of symbolic meaning to the perps."

Jesse waited.

"Obviously they wanted him found," Suitcase said.

"But why hanging?" Peter Perkins said.

Suitcase shook his head. Jesse looked at Molly. She shook her head.

"Perk," Jesse said. "Any theories?"

Perkins shook his head.

"Okay," Jesse said. "It looks like, for now, we wait for the forensics report."

"Unless something turns up," Suitcase said.

"Unless that," Jesse said.

D ix was as shiny as he always was. His white shirt was crisp with starch. His slacks were sharply creased. His shoes were polished. His thick hands were clean. His nails were manicured. He was bald and clean shaven, and his head gleamed. The white walls of his office were bare except for a framed copy of his medical degree and one of his board certification in psychiatry. Jesse sat at one side of the desk, and Dix swiveled his chair to face him. After he swiveled, he was motionless, his hands resting interlaced on his flat stomach.

"I'm making progress on the booze," Jesse said.

Dix waited.

"I quit for a while and it seemed to give me more control of it when I went back."

"Enough control?" Dix said.

Jesse thought about it.

"No," he said. "Not yet."

"But some," Dix said.

"Yes."

Dix was still.

"If I can control it," Jesse said, "life is better with alcohol. Couple of drinks before dinner. Glass of wine with dinner. Civilized."

"And without it?" Dix said.

"A lot of days with nothing to look forward to," Jesse said.

"Behavior can be modified," Dix said.

"In terms of drunks," Jesse said, "I'm not sure that's politically correct."

"It's not," Dix said. "But it's been my experience."

"So I'm not fooling myself."

"You may or may not be," Dix said. "It's possible that you're not."

"Day at a time," Jesse said.

Dix smiled.

"Now," Jesse said, "to my other problem."

Dix waited.

"I've met a woman," Jesse said.

Dix was still.

"Like the perfect woman," Jesse said.

Dix nodded slightly.

"She's good-looking, smart, very sexual. Even profession-ally—she's a private detective. Used to be a cop."

Dix nodded. It seemed to Jesse almost as if he were approving.

"She's tough. She can shoot. She's not afraid. And she's a painter, too. Oils and watercolors, not houses."

"Anyone else in her life?" Dix said.

"She's divorced, like me, and she might still be a little hung up on her ex."

"Gee," Dix said.

Jesse grinned at him.

"Like me," Jesse said.

Dix was quiet. The only window in the small room opened onto a budding tree against a blue sky. They looked almost like trompe l'oeil painting. When he was in this room with Dix, everything seemed remote to Jesse.

"Which is, of course, the problem."

"She can't let go of her ex-husband?" Dix said.

"I can't let go of Jenn," Jesse said.

"Because?"

"Two possibilities," Jesse said. "I still love her, or I'm pathological."

Dix smiled again without speaking.

"Or both," Jesse said.

"The two are not mutually exclusive," Dix said.

"But I feel like I love Sunny, too. That's her name, Sunny Randall."

"One can have feelings for more than one person," Dix said.

"And how does one resolve those feelings," Jesse said.

"If they need to be resolved," Dix said, "one would talk to one's shrink about them."

"Well, something needs to be resolved," Jesse said. "I can't just live with both of them."

"There may be other options," Dix said.

"Like what?"

"We'll have to explore that," Dix said. "Is Jenn with anyone else at the moment."

"Jenn is usually with someone else at the moment."

"Are you attempting to be monogamous with Sunny?"

"We haven't talked about that yet."

"Is she with anyone else at the moment?" Dix said.

"I don't think so."

Dix was silent. Jesse was silent. The faux-looking trees stirred in the light breeze outside the window.

Then Jesse said, "Are you trying to inject a note of sweet reason into this discussion?"

"And me a licensed shrink," Dix said. "How embarrassing."

Molly Crane came into Jesse's office as he was making coffee. She carried a yellow cardboard folder.

"Forensics report is in," she said. "I organized it for you and put it in a folder."

"You wouldn't consider living with me, would you?" Jesse said.

"Maybe," Molly said. "I'll discuss it with my husband."

She put the folder on the desk. Jesse poured water into the coffeemaker and turned it on.

"Any surprises?" he said.

"A little one," Molly said. "They ID'd the body."

Jesse sat at his desk.

"Anybody we know?" he said.

Molly smiled.

"Walton Weeks," Molly said.

"The talk-show guy?"

"Uh-huh."

"Jesus Christ," Jesse said.

"Can you say national media?"

Jesse nodded.

"Walton Weeks," he said.

Molly nodded.

"Well," she said, "if somebody had to go."

"I never listened to him," Jesse said.

Molly said, "I never agreed with him about anything."

"Doesn't make him a bad person," Jesse said.

Molly smiled.

"No," she said. "Come to think of it, I agree with my husband about very little, either."

"Let's not share any personal views with the national media."

Molly drew herself to attention.

"Protect and serve," she said.

"That would be us," Jesse said.

He picked up the yellow folder and looked at the cover. Molly had labeled it WALTON WEEKS. Jesse sighed.

"It'll be worse than the serial killings," Molly said.

"The media? Yes, it will. This guy's a national figure."

"What was he doing here?" Molly said.

"Molly," Jesse said. "I just found out who he is."

"The question was rhetorical," Molly said.

"For now," Jesse said.

He opened the folder and began to read. Molly watched him for a moment. Then she went to the coffeepot, got two mugs, poured the now-brewed coffee into each. She put one mug on Jesse's desk and took the other one with her to the front desk.

*An orgy would sound boring,* Jesse thought, *if it was described in a forensics report.*

White male, five feet eleven inches, two hundred three pounds. Appeared to be about fifty. Victim was overweight, and appeared out of shape. No evidence of a struggle. Abrasions on body appeared postmortem.

*Probably when they moved him and strung him up.*

Cause of death, three .32-caliber bullets. Any one of which would have done it. The victim had bled to death. Had been dead probably two days before the body was hung from the tree.

*Nice call, Perk.*

Fingerprint ID established that the victim was Walton Wilson Weeks, age fifty-one. Jesse wondered if they had estimated his age before they ID'd him. There was evidence of liposuction on his belly and buttocks.

*Vanity, Walton—vanity, vanity.*

The phone rang. It was Healy.

"Walton Weeks?" Healy said.

"So quick," Jesse said. "I'm just reading the forensics myself."

"I'm the homicide commander of the state police," Healy said. "Commonwealth of Massachusetts."

"Oh yeah," Jesse said. "You know everything."

"Walton Fucking Weeks?"

"Middle name is Wilson," Jesse said.

"Walton Fucking Wilson Fucking Weeks?" Healy said.

"Yes."

"Hanging from a tree limb in Paradise, Massachusetts?"

"Talk about a public figure," Jesse said.

"He's got a national television show," Healy said. "A national radio show. A national newspaper column."

"Is that as important as being a state police captain?" Jesse said.

"No. But it's close. They're going to swamp you."

"Maybe not," Jesse said.

"Weeks was a big supporter of the governor," Healy said.

"The one who wants to be president?"

"Yeah. That one."

"So he's going to be all over this," Jesse said.

"And me," Healy said. "And you."

"That'll be an asset."

"I'll help you all I can, and I'll keep him out of your way as much as I can," Healy said.

"Explain to him about you being a state police captain," Jesse said.

"I don't know," Healy said. "He might faint dead away."

"Yeah," Jesse said. "I feel a little woozy myself."

"Everyone does," Healy said.

"Got any idea what Walton Weeks was doing around here?" Jesse said.

"Not yet."

"Any other helpful things to tell me?"

"Hey," Healy said. "This is your case. I don't want to overstep."

"Which means you don't know shit," Jesse said.

"Much less than that," Healy said.

The smell of the harbor drifted into Jesse's condo through the open French doors that led to the small balcony. Jesse carried a tall scotch and soda to the balcony. He stood and looked at the harbor. Darkness had begun to settle but had not yet enveloped. He could still see Paradise Neck across the harbor, and Stiles Island off the tip of the neck. He sipped the scotch. Faintly, to his left, he could hear the music and chatter from the Gray Gull restaurant on the town wharf. In the harbor a couple of the boats at mooring were lighted and people were having cocktails. He sipped his scotch. Cocktail hour. He was starting to feel centered. He thought about Sunny Randall. He'd see her this weekend. Walton Weeks permitting. There were worse things than being in love with two women. Better than being in love with none. Sunny was perfect for him. Jenn was not. Jenn was still the promiscuous, self-absorbed adolescent she was too old to be. She'd cheated on him in Los Angeles. She'd cheated on him here. Maybe it was time to stop believing the promises. He finished his scotch and made another. In the darkening harbor, a flat-bottomed, square-backed skiff was being rowed toward a big, brightly lit Chris Craft cabin cruiser. A man was rowing. A woman sat in the stern. He thought about Sunny naked. It pleased him, but it led him to think of Jenn naked, which led him to think of her naked with other men. He heard a guttural sound. Like an animal growling. It came, he realized, from him. With the drink in his left hand, he made a gun out of his right forefinger and thumb, and dropped the thumb and said, "Bang." Below him, in the harbor, the tide was coming in. The rowboat was making slow progress against it. He drank some scotch. If Sunny committed to him, he knew she'd be faithful. They'd both be faithful. If he committed to Sunny. Which he wished he could do. But he couldn't. *What the hell is wrong with Jenn? Why is she like that?* He shook his head and drank some scotch. *Wrong question. Why can't I let her go?* Jesse's glass was empty. He went for a refill. As he poured he looked at his picture of Ozzie Smith. *Best glove I ever saw.* He remembered, as he did every day, the way his shoulder had hit the ground one night in Pueblo, trying to turn a double play, getting taken out by a hard slide. *I'd never have been Ozzie, but I'd have made the Show.* He walked back to the balcony. The rowboat had reached the Chris Craft. It was empty now, riding gently at the end of a tether line. *I'm a pretty good cop . . . except for getting fired in L.A. . . . I been a pretty good cop here . . . if I don't booze it away . . . I do booze it away, I'll have to become a full-time drunk . . . I got nothing else I know how to do.* Walton Weeks was going to be a hairball. He could feel it. Cameras, tape recorders, notepads, microphones, CNN, Fox, the networks, local news, Court TV, the *Globe,* the *Herald, The New York Times. People, US, The National Enquirer . . .* Reporting live from Paradise, Massachusetts, this is Every Prettyface. Ringling Bros., Barnum & Bailey. Jenn was an investigative reporter now. Not many weather girls made that jump. Jesse was pretty sure she had made it on her back. Walton Weeks would bring her out. He knew her. She'd be looking for an exclusive, an inside look, her special perspective. She'd use him if she could. He knew her. All he had left was being a cop. "I won't let her," Jesse said aloud. He drank, staring out at the harbor. There was no moon. It was too dark now to see the skiff. He held his glass up and looked through it at the still-bright light of the party boat. Pale amber. Clear ice. Thick glass. He took in some sea-scented spring night air. *Last drink. Then I'll make a sandwich. Maybe have a beer with it. Go to bed.* He finished the drink slowly, standing in the dark on the balcony. He listened to the harbor water moving gently below his balcony.

"I won't give her up," he said.

Then he turned and went in and closed the doors behind him.

The reporters were gathered in a press tent in the parking lot in back of the Town Hall, to the side of the DPW garage. Several portable toilets had been set up. The equipment trucks had filled most of the parking lot behind the supermarket. More portable toilets. There was a press briefing scheduled each morning at nine a.m. in the Town Hall auditorium. Molly was to do the briefing.

"This is blatant sexism," she said.

"You're the only one I trust in front of the press."

"How about you?"

"I'm the chief," Jesse said.

"For crissake," Molly said, "we have nothing to tell them."

"True," Jesse said.

"So what am I supposed to say?"

"Tell them we have nothing to tell them," Jesse said.

"It may be weeks before we have anything to tell them," Molly said. "What do I do up there every day?"

"Charm them," Jesse said. "Wear the full gun belt, makes you look really cute."

"You are a sexist pig," Molly said.

"Maybe you could have your hat on at a rakish angle," Jesse said.

"Fuck!" Molly said and left the office.

Suitcase Simpson came in with a notebook.

"What's up with Molly," Suit said. "I think she tried to bite me when I passed her in the hall."

"Gee," Jesse said. "I can't imagine."

Simpson shrugged.

"I got some preliminary stuff on Weeks," he said.

Jesse said, "Okay," and nodded toward one of the chairs.

"I'll type this all up nice on the computer," Simpson said. "But for now I'll give you the, ah, salient facts."

"You're taking courses again," Jesse said.

"Just one night a week," Simpson said. "In a few years I'll get my associate's degree."

"Onward and upward," Jesse said. "Whaddya got that's salient?"

"He was born in 1953 in Gaithersburg, Maryland. Went to high school there. Got a job after high school as a disc jockey, had a series of radio jobs, went to D.C. as a weatherman. Ended up with a talk show. Talk show got syndicated. And . . . you know. The rest is history. When he died he had a show on national cable two nights a week."

"*Walton's Week*," Jesse said.

"Right, and five days a week on national radio," Suit said.

"*Walton Weeks: How It Is.*"

"You listen to him?" Suit said.

"No."

"He's written a coupla books," Suit said. "I ordered them online."

Jesse nodded.

"He's been married three times."

"Was he married at his death?" Jesse said.

"Far as I know. Lorrie Weeks."

"So where is she?" Jesse said.

"Haven't found her address yet."

"But why hasn't she showed up here?" Jesse said. "It's national news."

Suit shrugged.

"How about the other wives?" Jesse said.

"Got names," Suit said. "Haven't found addresses yet."

"Kids?"

"Not that I know about," Suit said.

"Famous guy dies publicly, and no one shows up," Jesse said.

"Not quite."

"Somebody?" Jesse said.

"Bodyguard called in," Suit said.

"Bodyguard," Jesse said.

"Guy named Conrad Lutz."

"Conrad did a hell of a job," Jesse said. "You got an address for him?"

"Langham Hotel," Suit said. "In Boston. He was there with Weeks."

"Post Office Square," Jesse said.

"I guess," Suit said. "Molly told him to come in for an interview."

"When?"

"ASAP," Suit said.

"Press will swarm him," Jesse said.

He shrugged.

"But that's what they do," he said.

"You think Weeks was afraid of something?" Suit said. "You know, having a bodyguard?"

"He was a famous man who annoyed a lot of people," Jesse said.

"Be good to know who they were," Suit said.

"Maybe Conrad will know," Jesse said.

J esse," the voice on the phone said, "it's Daisy Dyke. I need
you to come up here."

"Business?" Jesse said.

"Yes, but could you come by yourself, like quiet?"

"Sure. I'll walk over."

"Thank you."

When he went out of the station house, he had to push
his way through the press.

"I'm going to lunch," Jesse said.

He said nothing else and ignored all questions. It was a
ten-minute walk to Daisy's Restaurant. Three of the reporters

tagged after him. Daisy met him at the door. She was a big, strong-looking woman with blond hair and a red face.

"We ain't open yet," she said to the three reporters. She let Jesse in and locked the door.

"I don't know what to do," Daisy Dyke said. "I figured I should talk to you first."

"Okay," Jesse said.

"There's a woman in my Dumpster," Daisy said.

"A woman," Jesse said.

"She's dead," Daisy said.

Jesse took a deep breath and tipped his head back and stretched his neck.

"You know how she died?" Jesse said.

"God, no," Daisy said. "But she's got blood on her."

"I'm going to have to look," Jesse said. "And then we're going to have to get her out of there. And then we're going to have to . . ." Jesse spread his hands. ". . . investigate."

"I know. I'm just worried about the fuckheads in the press ruining my business," Daisy said.

"We'll sneak as long as we can," Jesse said.

"But eventually they'll have to find out," Daisy said.

"Day at a time," Jesse said. "First, you take them some kind of nice snack, and let them sit at the sidewalk tables and eat it."

"I made some rhubarb scones this morning," Daisy said.

"Good. Give them that with coffee, and I'll slide out the back door and look at the woman."

"I gotta give them more than one scone?" Daisy said.

"Yes," Jesse said and walked to the back door.

He waited there until he heard Daisy open the front door. Then he went out the back.

She was there, on her back in the Dumpster, surrounded by garbage. The blood had dried black on her chest. There was no blood visible anyplace else. Not very old. Maybe thirty. Her clothes were expensive and she had probably been good-looking. Now she was not good-looking. He clenched his jaw and opened her blouse. There were bullet holes. He shook his head. Somebody else could count them. He closed her blouse again and wiped his hands on his pants.

"Dead for a while," Jesse said to no one.

He glanced at the restaurant and shrugged and took out his cell phone.

9

Suitcase Simpson was the first to arrive, walking up the alley behind the restaurant.

"I parked behind the market," he said.

He looked at the body in the Dumpster.

"You tell how she died?"

"Shot in the chest," Jesse said.

"Why we sneaking around?"

"Stalling the press."

"Soon as the ME truck shows up, they'll spot it," Suit said. "They ain't going to park and sneak in."

"Secure the scene," Jesse said. "I'm going to talk with Daisy."

"I got no tape with me," Suit said. "It's in the car."

"Suit," Jesse said. "Just don't let anyone fuck with the body, okay?"

"Oh," Suit said. "Secure like that."

Jesse nodded and went back into the restaurant. The two waitresses were setting the tables for lunch. Daisy stood with her arms folded, glaring out through the front window at the reporters drinking her coffee and eating her scones.

"Fucking vultures," she said.

"Without them you got no morning paper," Jesse said.

"They should mind their own business," Daisy said.

"We are their business," Jesse said. "You got a murder victim in your Dumpster, Daisy."

"Well, you know," Daisy said, "I sort of figured she didn't jump in there for a nap."

"We can stall the press for an hour or two maybe. But they're going to know."

Daisy nodded, and kept nodding as she stared out her window.

"It's just a crime scene," Jesse said. "You might want to close the place today. By tomorrow you'll be old news."

Daisy kept nodding, her thick arms folded over her considerable chest, her body rocking slightly.

"You might not want to be too colorful," Jesse said.

"Like what?"

"Like maybe not introduce yourself as Daisy Dyke, for instance."

"I like that name. I'm proud of it."

"No reason not to be. But it makes a nice headline, and reporters got space to fill."

"Even though I don't know nothing about the murder."

"Even though," Jesse said.

"Fuck them," Daisy said.

"Good point," Jesse said.

Daisy went to the front door and opened it and said, "Hey, scumbags, there's a dead body out back of the restaurant."

The reporters looked up. Daisy jerked a thumb toward the rear of the building.

"In the Dumpster," she said.

Then she took a small sign off the inside doorknob and put it on the outside and shut the door. The sign said CLOSED.

J esse sat in his office with Suitcase Simpson watching Daisy Dyke on the noon news.

"You bet I'm a lesbian," Daisy said. "Married to a lesbian, and proud to be from Massachusetts."

"So much for low profile," Suit said.

The phone rang. Jesse clicked off the television.

On the phone, Molly said, "Ms. Randall for you, Jesse."

"Hold on a second," Jesse said.

He looked at Suit.

"It's Sunny Randall," he said to Suit. "We'll probably talk dirty on the phone and you're too young."

Suit shook his head.

"At your age," he said, and stood and left the office.

"Put her on," Jesse said to Molly.

"Shall I stay on the line?" Molly said.

"Jesus," Jesse said. "This is like living in a frat house."

"I'll take that as a no," Molly said.

In a moment he heard Sunny Randall's voice.

"Walton Weeks?"

"Walton Fucking Weeks," Jesse said.

"And somebody else," Sunny said. "Are they connected?"

"Don't know. ME is still thinking about it."

"Are we a little busy," she said, "up there in Paradise?"

"Actually, right now we're marking time and fending off the press."

"I saw Daisy Dyke on television," Sunny said.

"Her finest hour," Jesse said. "You're home?"

"Yes."

"Where you been?"

"Los Angeles," Sunny said. "Tidying up the loose ends on the Erin Flint business."

"Cronjager says he can tie Moon Monaghan to the killings out there."

"Yes."

"Buddy Bollen's in witness protection," Jesse said.

"I know."

"You see your agent friend?" Jesse said.

"Tony Gault? I did."

"You go shopping with him?"

"On Rodeo Drive?" Sunny said.

Jesse said, "Yeah."

"Maybe in the Jere Jillian boutique?"

"Yeah."

"Maybe in the fitting room?" she said.

Sunny's voice seemed to develop overtones as she talked.

"Uh-huh."

"No," she said. "Why do you ask?"

"I'm the chief of police, I gather information."

"We aren't going steady, are we?" Sunny said.

"Not quite," Jesse said.

"We could," Sunny said.

"You bet," Jesse said.

"As soon as you're clear of Jenn, and I'm clear of Richie."

"Right after that," Jesse said.

"Still," Sunny said. "We might wish to relive some of those golden moments from the fitting room at Jere Jillian."

"We do wish to do that," Jesse said.

"I'll come up tonight," Sunny said. "About seven?"

"Should we have a drink first?"

"Oh, you civilized devil," Sunny said. "You're not going to jump me in the living room?"

"Probably not," Jesse said. "Bring Rosie."

"Of course," Sunny said. "I'm pretty sure I love you."

"Better than Richie?"

"Oops," Sunny said.

"Yeah. And then there's Jenn."

"Oops again," Sunny said.

They were quiet for a moment, listening to nothing on the phone line between them.

"Doesn't mean we won't have a nice night," Sunny said.

"No," Jesse said. "It doesn't."

"One night at a time," Sunny said.

L ate night?" Molly said.

Jesse nodded.

"How's Sunny," Molly said.

She was sitting with Jesse in his office, a notebook open in her lap.

"Very good," Jesse said.

"I like her," Molly said.

"Me too," Jesse said.

"You want my opinion on the two of you?"

"No."

"I think you'd be perfect together," Molly said.

"What's in your notebook?" Jesse said.

Molly smiled, mostly to herself, and looked down at her notebook.

"ME found some interesting stuff," Molly said.

Jesse waited.

"They'll have a formal report for us later," Molly said, "but here's what they know now."

Jesse waited.

"Aren't you even going to say, 'What? What?'" Molly said.

Jesse looked at her.

"Okay," she said. "First off, the bullets that killed her match the ones that killed Weeks."

Jesse nodded.

"Second off, she was ten weeks pregnant."

Jesse nodded again.

"Third off," Molly said, "they did a DNA match. Weeks was the father."

"That all?" Jesse said.

"You bastard," Molly said. "No, that's not all. Fourth off, she was killed about the same time Weeks was."

"With the same gun," Jesse said. "While carrying his child."

"Perhaps the crimes are related," Molly said.

"Good thinking," Jesse said. "They have an ID on her?"

"No. Fingerprints aren't in the system."

"Or they are and the system lost them," Jesse said.

"Wow, that's cynical."

"I been doing this for a while," Jesse said.

"Oh, for heaven's sakes, Jesse. You're not much older than I am," Molly said.

"But a lot uglier," Jesse said.

"True," Molly said. "I called the Langham. They tell me Weeks had a one-bedroom suite and two other rooms."

"Who was in the other rooms?"

"Lutz the bodyguard," Molly said. "And a woman named Carey Longley."

"Get the bodyguard in here," Jesse said.

"He's coming in today," Molly said.

"Okay, get some pictures of her from Peter Perkins. We'll see if Lutz knows her."

"She doesn't look so good," Molly said.

"It's as good as she's going to," Jesse said.

Molly nodded. She closed her notebook and stood and walked to the door. With her hand on the knob, she stopped and turned and looked at him.

"You know I love you, Jesse."

"As much as your husband and four kids?" Jesse said.

"No. But you're next."

Jesse smiled.

"Close enough," he said.

"You deserve Sunny Randall," Molly said.

"Not Jenn?" Jesse said.

"You deserve to be happy."

"And you don't think Jenn will make me happy?"

"How's it been going so far," Molly said.

Jesse nodded slowly.

"Of course, you can tell me to mind my own business," Molly said.

"Mind your own business."

"No," Molly said.

She smiled at him and opened the door.

"I won't," she said, and went out.

Jesse was eating a ham-and-cheese sandwich on light rye when Molly came in.

"Lutz is here," Molly said.

Jesse took a bite of the half-sour pickle that Daisy Dyke always sent with her sandwiches.

"And your wife is on the phone."

Jesse chewed the bite of pickle and swallowed.

"Ex-wife," he said.

"So you say."

Jesse took in some air and let it out slowly.

"Hold Lutz for a few minutes," Jesse said. "I'll talk to Jenn."

Molly nodded. Jesse put his hand on the phone. Molly didn't leave. Jesse looked at her with his hand on the phone. Molly shook her head and left the office. Jesse picked up the phone.

"Hi," he said.

"I'm in your apartment," Jenn said. "You have to come right now."

Jesse nodded as if she could see him.

"Sort of a busy time right now, Jenn."

"A man raped me," she said.

Jesse felt it across his upper back and shoulders. His trapezius muscles bunched involuntarily.

"You need a doctor?" Jesse said.

"I need you."

"I'll be right there," Jesse said.

He stood, and took his gun from the desk and put it on his belt. Then he walked out through the station. Molly was at the front desk. A big man with a thick mustache and a shaved head sat waiting. Jesse assumed it was Lutz.

"Ask Mr. Lutz to wait," Jesse said to Molly.

She stared at him. He kept going out the front door of the station. It seemed to him that he moved inside some sort of soundless space that enveloped him as he drove.

Jesse's front door was locked. When he unlocked it, he discovered that the security chain was in place.

"It's me, Jenn," Jesse said through the small opening.

"Okay," Jenn said.

Her voice was small. She closed the door and slid the chain loose and opened it again. Jesse stepped in. Jenn backed away from him. She looked fine. Her makeup was in place. Her hair was smooth. She wore jeans that fit well and a white shirt open at the neck. *He didn't beat her up.* As he closed the door and turned toward her, she seemed to move farther from him. He went to the bar and sat on a stool in front of his big picture of Ozzie Smith.

"Tell me about it," he said.

She shook her head. She walked slowly to the window and looked out and then walked back toward the kitchen. She stopped near the kitchen door.

"I don't want to talk about it," Jenn said.

Jesse nodded. She walked to the hall leading to the bedroom and looked down it and turned and walked back to the kitchen door.

"Report it to the cops?" Jesse said.

She shook her head.

"I just finally got moved from weather girl to investigative reporter. It would ruin my credibility. You know what the press is like."

"I do," Jesse said.

"You know the guy?"

"No."

"When did it happen?" Jesse said.

"Sunday night."

"That's four days ago."

"Yes," Jenn said.

She walked to the front door and looked out through the sidelights. Jesse waited. After a time, Jenn turned back toward him.

"He's stalking me."

Again Jesse felt it across his shoulders. He was aware, against his hip, of the mild weight of his holstered gun.

"Is he here?" Jesse said.

Jenn seemed to jump a little.

"Here?"

"Did he follow you here?" Jesse said.

"No. I saw him outside my apartment this morning, so went out through the back cellar door and down the alley. I took a cab here."

"How long has he stalked you."

"I saw him near the station when I went in, the day after it happened. Yesterday, he was hanging around a shoot I was on in Natick. . . . What would you have done if he were here."

Jesse was quiet.

"I want to know," Jenn said.

"I would have seen to it," Jesse said, "that he never hurt you again."

Jenn nodded and folded her arms and leaned her back against the door.

"Would you kill him?"

"If I had to," Jesse said.

"I'd kill him," Jenn said. "I will kill him if I get a chance."

Jesse nodded.

"I need you to get me a gun."

Jesse nodded.

"And show me how to use it."

"I can do that," Jesse said.

"You know what the bastard was like?" Jenn said.

Jesse shook his head.

"He came into my apartment right behind me," Jenn said. "He had a gun. He stood there in my living room and pointed the gun at me and made me undress."

Jesse was very still.

"For crissake, stand there and undress," Jenn said. "Take off all my clothes, squirm out of my pantyhose, in front of a total fucking stranger."

Jesse waited. Jenn was barely talking to him.

"And then I'm standing there completely undressed, nothing on, and the fucking sonovabitch couldn't get it up."

Jesse nodded.

"I had to stand there naked and watch him fondle himself until he was hard enough."

Jenn's breathing was heavy now, and short. Jesse listened to the interior sound his own breath made going in and out. He was breathing harshly, too.

"Then he made me lie on the floor and he did it. On the floor. He jammed it in and pushed hard and called me names and told me I liked it rough."

Jesse nodded.

"It hurt," Jenn said.

"Did you see a doctor?"

"No."

"I can take you," Jesse said.

"No."

"How can I make it better?"

"Find him and kill him."

Jesse nodded. Jenn stood and tried to control her breathing.

"I'll find him," Jesse said.

"And kill him?"

"Can you work with a sketch artist?" Jesse said.

Jenn shrugged.

"Could you pick him out of a mug book?" Jesse said.

Jenn shrugged again.

"I have to stay with you," Jenn said. "You have to protect me."

Jesse nodded.

"I'll protect you," he said.

"All the time."

"There'll be someone with you," Jesse said, "all the time."

"You?"

"Me or somebody good."

"I want you," Jenn said.

"We'll figure something out," Jesse said. "We'll make it work."

Jenn's lying down in the bedroom," Jesse said on the phone.
"Can you talk with Lutz?"

"Sure," Molly said.

"See if he can ID the woman," Jesse said. "Find out what
Weeks was doing in town. Why Weeks needed a bodyguard,
that kind of thing."

"I can do that," Molly said.

"Thank you."

"And run the daily briefing, and the front desk."

"I know you can."

"And take care of my husband and four kids."

"Of course," Jesse said.

"I am woman, hear me roar."

"It won't be forever," Jesse said.

"What are you going to do about Jenn?" Molly said.

"I don't know yet."

"Maybe it will be forever."

"No. I'll figure it out."

"I'm a woman, Jesse. I sympathize maybe more than you can imagine with Jenn. I want her safe, and I want the rapist where he should be."

"Which might be in the ground," Jesse said.

"I would have no problem with that," Molly said. "As long as you came out of it okay."

"Thank you."

"I care about you, Jesse, and I can imagine how you feel," Molly said. "Yes, we can get by in the short run, probably. But this department won't function without you."

"Yes."

"Especially now."

"Yes."

"Plus, you can't find the rapist for her if you are home watching her all day."

"Sometimes I'll be at the studio watching her," Jesse said.

"You know what I mean," Molly said.

"I do."

"And we can't spare anybody, Jesse. Not now, not with the two murders and the goddamned press. Plus, the governor's office calls every day. And some congressman."

"I know."

"And what are you going to do about Sunny Randall?" Molly said.

"I don't know."

"Jesse," Molly said. "This is a fucking mess."

"Thank you for noticing," Jesse said.

"I want to ask you a bad question," Molly said.

"Why should today be different," Jesse said.

The line was silent for a moment.

"Do you completely believe her?" Molly said.

"That is a bad question," Jesse said.

"I know."

Again the line was silent.

Then Jesse said, "Maybe not completely."

After a time, Molly said, "Will you be there if I need you?"

"Yep."

"I'll talk with Lutz," Molly said. "And call you back."

"Talk about phoning it in," Jesse said.

He hung up and stood and walked past his picture of Ozzie to the French doors and opened them and went out and stood on the balcony and looked at the harbor and thought.

T his is absolutely insane," Sunny Randall said.

"I know," Jesse said.

"She and I can't be together," Jenn said.

"Of course not," Jesse said.

He was sitting on a stool at the bar in his living room in front of his picture of Ozzie Smith. Jenn sat in a chair to his left, near the bedroom corridor. Sunny sat in a chair to his right. *We're even sitting in a triangle,* Jesse thought. The phone rang. He picked it up and looked at the display. It was Molly. He answered.

"Jesse, there's a guy here from the governor's office," Molly said. "Looking for you."

"Tell him I'm not available now."

"He won't like that," Molly said.

"I can't worry, right now," Jesse said, "about what people like."

"I'll try to handle it," Molly said.

"Thanks, Moll."

"But I'm not the chief of police," Molly said.

"Do what you can," Jesse said. "I'll be there when I can be there."

He hung up and looked at the two women. Neither of them said anything. It was late morning, and the sun coming through the French doors made a long, bright parallelogram on the living-room floor. Jesse picked up an empty highball glass from the bar. It was made of thick glass and had a nice heft to it.

"I need a drink," Jesse said.

Neither woman spoke.

"Probably needed too many drinks in my life," Jesse said.

The women stayed quiet. Jesse smiled without happiness. He turned the empty glass slowly in both hands.

"Booze aside," he said, "there are, as far as I can tell, three things in life that matter to me. Jenn, Sunny, and being a cop. Things have not gone well with us, Jenn. But because I can't quite let you go, things aren't going as well as they should with you, Sunny."

"In fairness," Sunny said, "there is, of course, Richie."

Jesse nodded.

"In fairness," Jenn said. "There are a lot of things."

ROBERT B. PARKER

"Both of you," Jesse said, "matter more to me than anything, except my job, and I seem unable to do my job if I don't ask you to do something that is probably unfair to both of you."

"Which would make you, in some sense, oh-for-three," Sunny said.

"Yes, I cannot allow Jenn to be unprotected. I cannot allow her rapist to walk around free and easy. And I cannot protect her or find her rapist and remain a good chief of police."

"Which was what saved you when you came east from L.A.," Jenn said. "Alone."

"It's what I have," Jesse said.

"In some odd way," Jenn said, "you have both of us."

"I know."

"Which also means you have neither of us," Sunny said.

"I know."

The sun had gotten higher, and the long rectangle of sunlight on the living-room floor had shortened.

"Do you love him?" Sunny said to Jenn.

Jenn shook her head.

"I don't know how to answer that," she said. "I do know that I cannot imagine a life without Jesse in it."

"To protect you?" Sunny said.

Jenn nodded.

"I know it looks like that," she said. "And I probably deserve that it does. But it's always that way. With him.

Without him. With someone else. I cannot imagine a life without him in it."

"I understand that," Sunny said.

"Can you protect me?" Jenn said.

"You mean am I any good?" Sunny said.

"You're a woman."

"Who better?"

Jenn looked at Jesse.

"She can protect you," he said. "And she can find your rapist."

Jenn looked back at Sunny.

"Would you?"

"Rape is something men can understand," Sunny said. "But women not only understand it, they feel it in their viscera. In terms of what happened to you, Jesse will never know what we know right now."

"Yes," Jenn said.

"Right now the most important thing in the room is what happened to you," Sunny said. "I will protect you until the sonovabitch is in jail or dead. Either one."

"Do you have a gun?" Jenn said.

Sunny opened her purse and took out a short revolver.

"And you can shoot?" Jenn said.

"Quite well," Sunny said.

Jenn began to cry. Sunny put the gun away and went and sat on the arm of Jenn's chair and put her arm around Jenn's shoulders. Jenn turned a little and pressed her face against Sunny's rib cage and cried harder. Sunny patted her.

"You're going to be fine," she said. "We're going to do just fine together."

Jesse felt as if he were intruding. He sat silently on his bar stool and rolled the empty glass in his hands.

Jenn and Sunny left together. Jesse sat at the bar for a time after they left, rolling the empty glass in his hands. The scent of their perfumes remained, commingling in the quiet room. The sun splash on the floor was gone. Jesse put the glass down, took his gun from a drawer and put it on, looked around the silent room for a moment. Inhaled. And went to the station.

"I got Lutz in the squad room," Molly said. "Waiting patiently."

"Good," Jesse said.

"And I've got the jerk from the governor waiting in your office."

"Not patiently," Jesse said.

"No."

Jesse started down the corridor.

"Where you going?" Molly said.

"Squad room."

Molly stared at him for a moment, and opened her mouth, and shut it and said nothing.

Jesse opened the door to the squad room.

"I'm Jesse Stone," he said.

Lutz stood. They shook hands. He had a hard handshake.

"Con Lutz," he said.

They sat. Lutz picked up a foam coffee cup from the conference table and drank some.

"Must be something genetic," Lutz said. "I've never had good coffee in a police station."

"You ever on the job?" Jesse said.

"Baltimore," Lutz said.

"Molly show you the pictures?"

"Yep. It's Carey Longley."

"Tell me about her," Jesse said.

"Walton's assistant. Been with him about a year."

"They an item?" Jesse said.

"You mean did they fool around?"

"Yeah."

"I ain't here to gossip about Walton," Lutz said, "or bad-mouth him, either. I worked for him eight years."

"Bodyguard."

"Yeah."

"Where were you this time?" Jesse said.

Lutz looked into his coffee cup for a moment. He shook his head.

"They went out without me," he said.

"Deliberately?"

"Yeah. Walton told me to take the night off. He said he and Carey were going out."

"That unusual?" Jesse said.

"Yes, he liked me to stay with him."

"They say where they were going?" Jesse said.

"No."

"She was ten weeks pregnant," Jesse said. "Weeks was the father."

Lutz looked at the surface of his coffee again.

"Okay," he said. "That takes it out of the realm of gossip, I guess."

"They an item?"

"Sure. A hot one. She was his girlfriend for a while before he hired her. I figured they were going off for some sort of romantic something, you know?"

"Anything wrong with the relationship?" Jesse said.

"Just that he had a wife," Lutz said. "Carey and Walton seemed fine."

"Wife know about Carey?"

"I don't think so. I mean, she knew he had an assistant. But I don't think she knew he was fucking her."

"He do this often?" Jesse said.

"Yeah. Walton liked women. He married three of them. He probably cheated on them all."

"What was he doing up here?"

Lutz shook his head.

"I don't know," he said. "Carey did all that stuff. I just protected him."

"You didn't know ahead of time?" Jesse said. "How'd you know if there would be security issues?"

"I wasn't the Secret Service," Lutz said. "Hell, Walton wasn't the president, either. If he was going someplace to give a speech or whatever, Carey would notify the local cops and they'd do what they thought they should do. I was just along to see that no one assaulted him on the sidewalk or whatever."

"Which you look like you can do," Jesse said.

"Which I can," Lutz said. "But tell you the truth, I think part of it was that Walton just liked having a bodyguard around. Good for his image."

"Ever any trouble."

"A few drunks," Lutz said. "A few protesters."

"Sometimes one and the same," Jesse said.

Lutz grinned.

"You got that right," he said.

"Any big trouble?"

"No."

"You and he get along?" Jesse said.

"Sure. Once we both got it that I was a bodyguard, not

somebody who runs errands, or makes coffee, or gets you a dinner reservation."

Jesse nodded.

"You have any idea why they ended up dead in my town?" Jesse said.

"No," Lutz said.

"Hate mail, death threats, warnings, anything like that?"

Lutz shook his head. "None that he shared with me."

"Who would he share them with?"

"Carey, maybe. She probably handled his personal mail. His manager would have handled the, you know, public-figure mail."

"You guard him twenty-four-seven?" Jesse said.

"No. In New York, he lives in a secure building. I'd drive him when he went out, but when he was home I was off duty, so to speak."

"When he traveled?" Jesse said.

"When he traveled I went with him. Stayed next door. But when he was in for the night, I was off."

"Know anything useful?" Jesse said.

"Guy's a bodyguard and his clients die," Lutz said, "it doesn't make him look good. Besides which, I worked for the guy eight years. So before I came up to see you, I checked a little. Nobody at the front door remembers getting them a cab. Nobody at the concierge desk remembers arranging anything. No car rental, no limo, no dinner reservation, no theater tickets, nothing."

"And people would remember," Jesse said.

"Walton was pretty well-known," Lutz said.

"Anyone remember them coming out of the hotel?"

"One doorman said he thought they headed up Franklin Street." Lutz smiled. "It wasn't Walton so much. Doorman says he was watching Carey's ass."

"Any people I should talk to about Weeks?" Jesse said.

"Sure," Lutz said. "I don't know everyone, but I can give you a few names to start with."

"You think of any Paradise connection?" Jesse said. "For either of them?"

"Only reason I ever heard of the place," Lutz said, "was that serial killing thing you had up here a while back."

"Either Carey or Walton ever mention the town?"

"Nope."

"You have any theory," Jesse said, "about why they died, or why they ended up here?"

"None," Lutz said.

"That makes two of us," Jesse said.

16

C ould you join me with the governor's guy?" Jesse said to
Molly as he walked to his office.

"Always best to have a witness," Molly said.

The man in Jesse's office didn't stand when they came in.
He was maybe fifty. He wore black wingtipped shoes, a dark
suit, a red tie, and a white shirt with a collar pin. His sandy
hair was newly cut and parted on the left.

"Richard Kennfield," he said. "From Governor Forbes.
Didn't she tell you I was waiting?"

"Officer Crane?" Jesse said. "Yes, she told me."

Jesse sat behind his desk and, pushing the chair back, put one foot on an open bottom drawer.

"And you chose to keep me sitting here for several hours?"

"Yes," Jesse said.

"Do you have an explanation?"

Jesse nodded. Molly remained standing by the door.

"I do," he said.

Kennfield waited. Jesse was silent.

"What is it?" Kennfield said after a while.

"I had police work to do," Jesse said.

"And you don't think police work includes talking to the representative of the chief executive of the state?"

"Nope."

"Are you being deliberately obtuse?" Kennfield said.

"I'm not sure it's deliberate," Jesse said. "What can I do for you?"

Kennfield paused for a moment and weighed his options. Then he shook his head slightly, puffed his cheeks a little, and blew some air out.

"Walton Weeks was a longtime supporter of Governor Forbes," Kennfield said.

Jesse nodded.

"The governor is very concerned about his murder."

Jesse nodded.

"We would like a full report on the death of Walton Weeks," Kennfield said. "And the progress of the investigation."

"Me too," Jesse said.

"Meaning?"

"Meaning I don't know any more than you do."

"We want progress reports," Kennfield said. "We want to know every step you're taking."

"I've got everybody in the department looking for the killer or killers. We haven't found him . . . or her . . . or them."

"And we want the state police involved," Kennfield said.

Jesse realized that Kennfield was checking off a mental list.

"I've been in touch with the homicide commander," Jesse said.

"We want the full resources of the state brought to bear on this investigation," Kennfield said. "We want you working hand in glove with Captain Healy."

"Sure," Jesse said.

"Now"—Kennfield checked off another mental point— "what is your theory of the case?"

"Same people that killed Weeks," Jesse said, "killed Carey Longley."

"Carey . . . ?"

"His assistant."

"Oh, yes," Kennfield said. "Because of the same murder weapon."

"Because of that," Jesse said.

"And what haven't you told the press?" Kennfield said.

"That Carey was ten weeks pregnant with Walton's kid."

"Pregnant?"

"Yep."

"Is that a holdback?" Kennfield said.

"No," Jesse said. "We hold back things that only the killer could know, so if someone knows it, it's a clue. The killer or killers could have known, or not known, and if they knew could have known or not known that it was Walton Weeks's child. No point in holding it back. Somebody knows it, it proves nothing."

"Then why didn't you tell the press?" Kennfield said.

"Saw no good reason to. There's Weeks's widow and Carey's next of kin to think about."

"Yes, it's best kept quiet," Kennfield said. "Lorrie Weeks is a very close friend of the governor, and she has always been as supportive as Walton was."

"I can't promise you," Jesse said. "It may become pertinent, and if so, I'll blab."

"That would not endear you to us."

Jesse nodded.

"We want your cooperation in this," Kennfield said.

Jesse nodded.

"And our cooperation with you can be very helpful."

Jesse nodded.

"You don't seem to care," Kennfield said.

"I don't," Jesse said.

"Perhaps we could change that," Kennfield said.

He stood and walked to the door. With the door half open, he turned back to Jesse.

"Is it something personal?" he said. "Do you dislike the governor?"

Jesse shook his head.

"I don't even know the governor," Jesse said. "It's you I dislike."

Kennfield stared for a moment at Jesse, then he turned and left.

"Wait until he gets to his car," Molly said.

"Why?"

Molly smiled.

"I gave him a parking ticket," she said.

Jesse smiled and raised his right hand and Molly high-fived him.

H ow's it going so far?" Jesse said on the phone.

"Fine," Sunny said. "She's taking a shower right now."

"You think this might be kind of bizarre?" Jesse said.

"If things get back to normal, it will get bizarre, I suspect," Sunny said. "Right now it's about sisterhood."

"She and Rosie get along?"

"Deeply bonded," Sunny said. "In fact, Rosie is sitting at the bathroom door as we speak, waiting for Jenn to come out."

"Jenn's never had a dog," Jesse said.

"Well, she seems to like Rosie, and Rosie likes her," Sunny said.

"Jenn's a lot of fun," Jesse said.

"Except when she's not," Sunny said.

"Except then," Jesse said. "I don't assume you've made much progress on the rapist."

"We're just getting ourselves comfortable together," Sunny said. "I haven't even asked her about it yet."

"Hard to investigate if you have to stay with her all the time."

"My friend Spike will help with the babysitting," Sunny said. "And helping me investigate might be good for her . . . and here she is, looking elegant in a large bath towel."

Jesse could feel the memory of Jenn in his stomach. She would come from the shower like that, and flip the towel and flash him.

"I need to talk with her," Jesse said.

Jenn said, "Hello?"

"You okay?"

"Yes."

"What can you tell me about Walton Weeks?"

There was a pause. Jesse knew Jenn's focus was deep but narrow. It would take her a minute to think of anything but her situation. Suitcase Simpson appeared at Jesse's door, saw that Jesse was on the phone, and paused. Jesse waved him away and he disappeared.

"Me?" Jenn said.

"You're in his business," Jesse said.

"Well, I know he's very successful," Jenn said.

"Uh-huh."

"And he's, let's see . . . He's got the weekly TV show."

"*Walton's Week,*" Jesse said.

"Clever, isn't it," Jenn said. "And he's got his daily radio show, and the syndicated column he does."

"It's in the *Globe* around here," Jesse said. "Is he right-wing, left-wing?"

"Oh, hell, Jesse. I don't know. You know I don't pay attention to stuff like that."

"Who would know?" Jesse said.

"Have you tried the Internet?" Jenn said.

"I'm looking for someone I can talk with."

"I don't . . ." She was silent while she thought. "I know." Her voice quickened. "My former news director, Jay Wade. He's a communications professor now, at Taft, you know, in Walford."

"I know."

"I could call him for you," Jenn said. "Arrange for you to see him."

"You and he are pals?"

"Sure, we worked together for two years, Jesse."

"And he was your boss?" Jesse said.

"Yes. He's the one gave me that Race Week feature."

Alone in his office with his feet on the desk, Jesse nodded silently.

"I can call him," Jesse said. "Thanks."

When they had hung up Jesse sat motionless for a while. *I wonder if Jay fucked her?* He shook his head. *Got to stop doing that.* He stood and went to the door of his office and stuck his head out and yelled.

"Suit."

been going through that list of names you got from the bodyguard," Suit said.

Jesse waited. Suit always admired Jesse's silence. Suit thought he himself talked too much. He wished he were silent like Jesse.

"Couldn't reach the manager," Suit said. "He's in New York. I left word to call me back."

"And when he doesn't?"

"I'll call him again."

Jesse nodded.

"The wives all got back to me."

"Two ex- and one current," Jesse said.

"Yeah." Suit looked at his list. "Two of them in New York. They still use his name. Lorrie Weeks is the current wife, and Stephanie Weeks is wife number two. Ellen Migliore, wife one, is remarried and lives in Italy. I haven't talked to her."

Jesse nodded.

"The other two were mostly interested in the estate, you know, the will and stuff. Current wife, Lorrie, was also interested in Carey Longley and how come she got killed."

"They have any idea what he was doing up here?"

"Nope. Current wife says he told her only that it was business, and he'd be gone a few days."

"He was gone more than a few days," Jesse said.

Suit nodded.

"Did that seem to bother her?" Jesse said.

"Nope."

"Why not?"

"Jesus, Jesse," Suit said. "She just lost her husband, I didn't want to press her hard right away."

Jesse nodded.

"She may have killed him," Jesse said.

"Jesus," Suit said. "You think so?"

"I don't know," Jesse said. "Neither do you. And there's nothing wrong with kind. But we need to know what we need to know."

Suit nodded.

"Everybody I talked to said they had no idea who killed him. They said he was controversial but not, you know, crazy."

"Threats?" Jesse said. "Hate mail?"

"They said they didn't know, that his office handled that stuff."

"Who's the office?" Jesse said. "Carey?"

"No, according to them she was strictly his personal assistant. His manager handled the, you know, business stuff."

"There's probably a lawyer in there someplace," Jesse said.

"No lawyer on your list," Suit said. "Maybe the manager's a lawyer, too."

"Maybe," Jesse said. "When you talk to them, see if there's a lawyer."

"Okay."

"Any of the wives coming up here?"

"I don't know," Suit said. "None of them said they were."

"Anybody been arranging for a funeral?" Jesse said.

"The wife," Suit said. "Soon as the ME releases the body."

"That would be Lorrie," Jesse said.

"Yeah."

Jesse nodded. They were quiet for a time.

Then Suit said, "There's stuff bothering me."

"Like not knowing who did it?" Jesse said.

"Yeah," Suit said. "That. But this guy's a big famous public figure, you know. And nobody knows why he's up here."

Jesse nodded.

"I mean, there's nothing in the papers about him going to give a speech. Guy as famous as him, you always see stuff in the papers. His bodyguard don't even know why he's here."

"Or says he doesn't," Jesse said.

"And another thing," Suit said. "I can't think of a way to attract more attention to this case. Kill them at the same time. Save the bodies. Then hang the famous one on a tree. And wait awhile, and put the other one in a Dumpster."

Jesse smiled.

"Surprise," he said. "The press is all over it."

"For crissake," Suit said. "It's like the guy wants publicity."

"That bothers me, too," Jesse said.

19

Jay Wade had longish blond hair that he combed straight back. His eyes behind the aviator-style glasses were pale blue. His jaw was firm.

"You still see Jenn?" he said.

"Yes."

"You two together again?"

"No."

"I'm sorry to hear that," Jay said.

Jesse nodded. Maybe Jay Wade had never slept with Jenn. Or maybe he had. He could feel the muscles in his shoulders and neck tighten. *Calm down. She's not my property.*

*If I were him, I'd have slept with her, too.* The muscles continued to bunch.

"Jenn thinks you can tell me about Walton Weeks," Jesse said.

Jay Wade nodded and leaned back in his chair with his hands clasped behind his head.

"Actually," Jay said, "I knew Walton a little. I was political editor for a station in Maryland when he was doing weather."

"Tell me about him," Jesse said.

Jay smiled.

"Well," he said. "Walton always had a good voice. People liked his voice. It projected well. He sounded like a guy from your neighborhood, but smarter. Walton always sounded smart."

"Was he?"

"You know," Wade said, "I don't know. When I knew him he was a damn weatherman, you know. I never thought much about him being smart or dumb. After I left Maryland, and he got to be a national figure—I mean, who knows who wrote that column or the little editorial set pieces on his TV show. He seemed quick enough on the call-ins and guest interviews."

"So he has some staff support in all of this."

"Sure."

"You wouldn't know any names?" Jesse said.

"No. I don't want to mislead you. I once knew Weeks in a casual workplace way twenty years ago."

Jesse nodded.

"Did he ruffle a lot of feathers?" Jesse said.

"You mean back when I knew him or in his national celebrity phase?"

"Either way."

"When I knew him everybody liked him. He was pleasant," Wade said. "Now that he is, or was, a national figure, yeah, he ruffled a lot of feathers."

"Conservative or liberal?" Jesse said.

"God, didn't you ever listen to him?" Wade said.

"No."

"My God, what do you do with yourself."

"Mostly I'm a cop," Jesse said. "When I have free time I follow baseball."

"Jenn told me you used to play," Wade said.

"Yep."

"And you got hurt."

"Yep."

"Tough," Wade said.

Jesse nodded.

"What about Walton Weeks?" he said.

"Walton's a libertarian," Wade said. "That probably brings him more in line with the right than the left. But basically he believed that government which governs least governs best. He believed in what he called the Eleventh Commandment."

"Leave everyone else the hell alone," Jesse said.

"Yeah. Guy like Walton Weeks," Wade said, "it often depends on who's ox he's goring, you know? When he was hammering the tax-and-spend big-government liberals, the conservatives loved him and the liberals hated him. Now we seem to have spend-and-no-tax big-government conservatives in power, and he's been hammering them, and now they are hating him. Maybe worse, because they feel betrayed."

"You agree with him?" Jesse said.

"Currently I've tended to. But the problem with Walton is that he puts principle ahead of results."

"Like?"

"Civil rights," Wade said. "He believed completely in integration but felt the government should not impose it."

"And you disagree," Jesse said.

"A lot of us disagree. You think integration would have happened without government imposition?"

"No," Jesse said.

"Then you disagree with Walton, too."

"Not enough to kill him," Jesse said.

"You think he was killed for political reasons?" Wade said.

"Just rattling all the doorknobs," Jesse said. "I heard he was a womanizer."

Wade grinned.

"He was married several times," Wade said. "Me too. Depends on your perspective. You, ah, interact with a lot of women and you could be a womanizer, or you could just be very popular."

Jesse tried not to think about Jenn.

"Walton interacted," Jesse said.

"Often. It was an open secret in the industry," Wade said. "Not that there was anything especially hypocritical about it. It's not like you preach against drugs and you're a junkie, or you preach celibacy and there's nudies of you on the Web."

"So there could be a jealous husband," Jesse said.

"Sure," Wade said.

*This is too close.* Jesse could hear himself breathing. *This is too close.*

20

The law office was in a storefront in a strip mall. Jenn stood in the doorway with her microphone. Her cameraman focused. Sunny stood behind him, watching. She had seen no sign of the stalker.

"Rolling," the cameraman said.

Jenn knocked on the door. It opened, but not very much.

"Attorney Marc LaRoche?" Jenn said.

Someone muttered something from behind the slightly open door.

"Channel Three, how do you respond to allegations that you have consistently failed to adequately represent female clients in divorce cases?"

Another mumble.

"No, sir," Jenn said, "it is our business. The public has a right to know."

There was something inaudible from behind the open door and then the door slammed shut. Jenn pounded on it.

"Attorney LaRoche," she shouted. "Why won't you address this issue? Attorney LaRoche?"

Jenn turned and looked into the camera, holding her microphone.

"Perhaps Attorney LaRoche has something to hide," Jenn said. "Perhaps not. Clearly he doesn't wish to speak with us. We'll stay on this until all the truth is told. We don't take no for an answer. Jenn Stone, Channel Three."

The cameraman pulled back for a wide shot that showed a sign in the window: ATTORNEY MARC LAROCHE. Jenn kept looking into the camera until the cameraman said, "Okay, Jenn." Then she lowered the mike and all three of them walked to the News 3 van.

"You gonna do a lead-in?" the cameraman said.

Jenn shook her head.

"No. John will do the lead-in from the anchor desk."

"Okay," the cameraman said, "then let's go home."

Back at the station, Jenn took the tape to the editing room and left it.

"We'll edit this afternoon," she said to Sunny. "Right now we need lunch."

Sunny smiled.

"I almost always need lunch," she said.

As they walked across the vast brick plaza in front of City Hall, Sunny said, "Any sign of our stalker?"

Jenn glanced around and shook her head.

"Does he show up some places more than others?" Sunny said.

"No," Jenn said. "I never know."

As they walked, Sunny watched the men they passed. A number of them looked at Jenn, and some of them looked at her. It meant little. Jenn was recognizable, and both of them looked good enough for men to glance at them anyway.

In the Parker House they sat at a window in the restaurant. When they had ordered, Jenn leaned forward.

"We need to talk about Jesse and us," Jenn said.

Sunny nodded.

"Do you love Jesse?" Jenn said.

Sunny sat back in her chair with her hands in her lap. She was quiet for a little while. Jenn waited, still leaning forward.

"When I'm with him," Sunny said.

"And when you're not?"

"I don't miss him as much as I would expect to."

"How much would you expect to?" Jenn said.

*Surprise, surprise,* Sunny thought. *She's not dumb.*

"As much, I guess, as I miss my ex-husband," Sunny said.

"Do you see him much?" Jenn said.

"He's remarried."

"Doesn't mean you can't see him," Jenn said.

"We share a dog," Sunny said. "I see him when he picks her up or drops her off."

"Why did you get divorced?" Jenn said.

"I'm not sure, I'm working on it."

"No, I meant your idea or his?" Jenn said.

"I guess it was mine."

Through the window Sunny could see a man standing outside King's Chapel with his hands in his pockets. He was looking toward the hotel. Sunny didn't know if he could see them through the window. It depended on how the glass was reflecting.

"Could that be our stalker?" she said to Jenn.

Jenn flinched momentarily, then turned to look at the man.

"No," she said, "that's not him."

"You're sure?" Sunny said.

Jenn nodded slowly.

"If it was him, I'd have that awful feeling."

The waitress brought their salads. Jenn picked up a scrap of red lettuce from hers and ate it.

"I guess it was my idea, too," Jenn said.

"To leave Jesse?"

"I left him."

"Why?"

"I always say it was his drinking, but it wasn't. His drinking got worse after I left."

"So what was it?"

Jenn shrugged.

"I was an actress," she said. "I had an affair with a producer."

"Was he going to make you a star?" Sunny said.

Jenn made a face.

"Something like that," she said. "When Jesse found out, he said he could forgive anything once."

"You promised never to do it again," Sunny said.

"Yes."

"But you did it again."

"Jesse couldn't really forgive it. He didn't rant and rave or anything. But . . . his drinking got away from him, I guess."

"So you divorced him."

"Actually, he divorced me. But it was my fault. By the time we divorced, he had no other choice."

"Do you know why you continued to cheat on him?"

"Yes, I've talked with shrinks about it until my tongue hurts. It's too boring to try and explain."

"I don't need to know," Sunny said. "You still using the same techniques?"

Jenn smiled.

"Fucking my way to the top?" she said.

Sunny shrugged. Jenn ate a crouton.

"It's worked great," Jenn said. "I just recently got promoted from weather girl."

Sunny smiled.

"Show-business opportunities are not unlimited in this market," she said.

"For sure," Jenn said.

"Did you come here because Jesse was here?" she said.

"Yes."

"You still love him?"

"I think so."

"But you still . . ."

"I'm still trying to fuck my way to the top," Jenn said.

"But . . ." Sunny said.

"Jesse is like your ex-husband, you know? I can't imagine life without him in it."

"But . . ."

"Almost anything I know that matters, I learned from him," Jenn said.

Sunny waited.

"I always needed to be somebody, and I always thought that what I had to offer was that I looked good and I could fuck," Jenn said.

Sunny smiled.

"Most of us can," Sunny said.

"But I do," Jenn said. "Jesse was always somebody, you know? He was always so self-sufficient and complete and . . . *somebody.*"

"Except for you and drinking," Sunny said.

"Yes," Jenn said. "I think I kind of liked the drinking. It was a weakness, made him more human, sort of."

"And you?"

Jenn smiled and nodded.

"I thought that was a weakness, too," Jenn said. "You've had some therapy."

"Yes."

"One of my shrinks said if it weren't for his weaknesses," Jenn said, "me and booze, he would have been too complete, too . . . Jesse. If it weren't for those weaknesses . . ."

"Of which you were one," Sunny said.

Jenn nodded.

"Of which I was one," she said. "Without those weaknesses, I probably couldn't have loved him."

Jenn moved her salad around with her fork, without eating any of it.

"How about you?" Jenn said to Sunny.

Sunny didn't answer right away. She was looking out the window at the corner by King's Chapel. The man was gone. She smiled without very much pleasure.

"Richie didn't have any weaknesses," she said.

**B**eing out of uniform," Suit said. "Does this mean I'm a detective?"

"No," Jesse said.

"If I was out of uniform and got a significant raise?" Suit said.

"Might," Jesse said.

They were in New York, walking up West 57th Street.

"We're going to see Walton Weeks's manager," Suit said.

"Tom Nolan," Jesse said.

"In hopes of detecting who killed Walton," Suit said.

"Yes."

"So how come, if I'm detecting, I'm not a detective?"

They crossed Sixth Avenue with the light.

"Department's not big enough to have detectives," Jesse said.

"So I do detective work for patrolman's pay," Suit said.

"Exactly," Jesse said.

They passed the back entrance to the Parker Meridien hotel across 57th Street.

"Who's going to be there?" Suit said.

"With Nolan? The widow, and as much of the staff as he can get together."

"Current widow."

"Yes."

"We going to talk about the broad being pregnant?" Suit said.

"We won't introduce the topic."

"You think they know?" Suit said.

"I mentioned it to the governor's man, Kennfield," Jesse said.

"And you figure he blabbed."

"Yes."

They turned into a narrow building on West 57th Street.

"And you kind of want to see if he blabbed to them," Suit said.

"I do," Jesse said.

"Always nice," Suit said. "If you think a guy's a jerk, and he confirms your suspicion."

"Always," Jesse said.

They rode the elevator to the penthouse and buzzed at the office door. A voice asked who they were.

"Chief Stone," Jesse said, "and Detective Simpson, from Paradise, Massachusetts."

Suit grinned.

"Detective Simpson," he murmured.

After a moment the door clicked open and they went in. A well-groomed young woman showed them through a short reception area and into Tom Nolan's office. It was a narrow room that stretched across the front of the building. A window wall looked out over a part of the West Side.

With seven people in the room, it was crowded. Nolan sat behind a semicircular desk on the left wall, facing the windows. Four people sat in chairs in front of the desk, with the windows at their backs. At the far end of the office was a small white piano. In between were too many small tables, extra chairs, hassocks, and floor lamps. Suit went and stood beside the windows. Jesse stood near Nolan's desk. Introductions were made: Lorrie Weeks, the current wife; Stephanie Weeks, the previous wife; Alan Hendricks, Weeks's researcher; Sam Gates, Weeks's lawyer.

"Ellen Migliore now lives in Italy," Nolan said. "So she isn't here. There are other, less prominent people in Walton's life, but I wasn't sure how deep you wanted me to go in assembling the group."

"Ellen Migliore is the first Mrs. Weeks?" Jesse said.

"Yes."

"This group is fine," Jesse said.

"As Mr. Nolan pointed out," Jesse said, "I'm the chief of police in Paradise, Massachusetts, where Mr. Weeks and Ms. Longley were killed. The large young man by the window is Detective Simpson."

Suit nodded gravely to the assemblage.

"First," Jesse said. "We are sorry for your loss."

"May I ask a question?" Gates asked.

"Sure."

"Paradise is a small town, is it not?"

"It is," Jesse said.

"How big a police force do you have?" Gates asked.

"Twelve," Jesse said. "Plus me."

"Isn't it usual for the state police to step in when there's a big crime and a small, perhaps inexperienced, force?"

"That's quite common," Jesse said.

"But not in this case?" Gates said.

"State police are standing by," Jesse said.

"But you're running the investigation," Gates said.

"Yes."

"This is a rather important murder," Gates said.

"They all are," Jesse said.

"Touché," Gates said. "Let me rephrase. This murder has created national attention."

"Murders," Jesse said.

"Of course, these murders have created national attention. Do you have the necessary resources?"

"We do," Jesse said.

"Well, you're confident," Gates said. "I'll give you that."

"Thanks," Jesse said.

"I assume you wish to ask us some questions," Tom Nolan said.

"I do," Jesse said.

He looked at Lorrie.

"You arranged burial."

"Yes."

"Private ceremony?"

"Yes, it's how Walton would have wished it."

"Back here," Jesse said.

"Yes. This was home for Walton and me," she said. "Mr. Lutz helped me with the arrangements."

"The girl, too?"

"It seemed only decent. No one on her side of things seemed to care."

"So you buried her back here, too," Jesse said.

"Yes, it seemed the simplest arrangement."

"Lutz took care of that, too," Jesse said.

"Yes."

"You might have had some formal moment," Stephanie said.

Lorrie gazed at her blankly.

"I was, am, in a state of some shock," she said finally.

Stephanie shrugged.

The two wives looked somewhat alike. Dark hair, good bodies, expensive clothes, expert makeup. To Jesse, Stephanie looked maybe twenty years older than Lorrie. Otherwise there was little to choose between them.

The two women looked at each other silently, until Lorrie spoke again.

"I was just so grief-stricken," she said. "I didn't know what I should do."

"Hard to know what to do in these situations," Jesse said.

"Oh God," Lorrie said. "This is so awful."

"I understand," Jesse said to Tom Nolan, "that you have no next of kin for Ms. Longley."

"No," Nolan said. "She didn't list any when we hired her. No one has appeared?"

"No."

"God," Nolan said, "it's all over the news. If there were parents or somebody, they must have heard."

"Weeks gets more attention," Jesse said.

Nolan nodded.

"Still," he said.

Jesse shrugged.

"Who inherits?" Jesse said.

"The estate has not been settled yet," Gates said. "And it's reasonably complicated. But there are substantial bequests to all three wives."

"Is there one person whose bequest is more substantial?" Jesse said.

"Lorrie receives the largest share."

"Anyone else in there but the wives?"

"There are small bequests to various staff members, and a modest bequest to Alan Hendricks."

Jesse looked at Hendricks. He was a handsome young man, with close-cropped hair and olive skin. He was taller than Jesse, and slender, with big black-rimmed glasses.

"You were Weeks's researcher," Jesse said.

"Yes. Walton was very active on the phone, but I did much of the fieldwork."

Jesse nodded. From his place by the window, Suit was taking notes. *If ever we have detectives . . .*

"What's happened to Weeks Enterprises?" Jesse said.

"TV and radio, we're doing a retrospective," Nolan said. "You know, the best of . . . same with the newspaper column."

"Then what?"

Gates stepped in.

"Once the estate is settled," Gates said, "we'll proceed in consonance with the wishes of the estate."

"Who is, in terms of the shows and the column?" Jesse said.

"Lorrie, unless there's something untoward."

"Such as?" Jesse said.

"A problem in settling the estate," Gates said. "Extended litigation. Walton Weeks is a public franchise, and like all such, the franchise depends on currency and continuity. If Walton Weeks were off the market for an extended time, his value would diminish substantially. For everyone."

"Do you plan to litigate?" Jesse said to Stephanie Weeks.

"No. She got him away from me fair and square," Stephanie said. "She's earned it."

Lorrie looked at Stephanie but said nothing.

"What are your plans?" Jesse said to Hendricks.

"I hope to continue Walton's legacy," Hendricks said. "In some capacity or other."

"Why all this interest in the estate?" Gates said.

"Just assembling information," Jesse said.

"You think his inheritance would be a motive?" Gates said.

"We've drawn no conclusions," Jesse said.

"Do you have a theory of the crime?"

"The same gun killed Walton Weeks and Carey Longley," Jesse said. "We speculate that it was used by the same person or persons."

"That's it?" Gates said.

"Yep. Anyone know why he was in Boston?"

No one answered.

"Mrs. Weeks?" Jesse said to Lorrie.

"Just said he was going up on business," Lorrie said.

"How long was he going to stay?"

"He didn't say."

"You didn't worry about it when he was gone for a while?"

"He was often gone for a while," Lorrie said. "Our marriage was not about keeping tabs."

"Did he do that when you were married to him?" Jesse said to Stephanie.

"Yes. Usually he was with a woman. Toward the end of our marriage the woman was her." Stephanie pointed at Lorrie with her chin.

"Oh, like you were Miss Stay-at-home Faithful," Lorrie said. "You were pretty busy yourself."

"Weren't we all," Stephanie said.

Lorrie reddened.

"Hendricks put a hand on her forearm.

"Ladies," he said. "Ladies. This isn't the time, ladies."

Everyone was silent. Jesse waited. No one spoke.

"Does anyone have any thought on who might have wanted to kill Walton Weeks and Carey Longley?"

No one spoke. Jesse waited.

Then Hendricks said, "Maybe somebody only wanted to kill one of them and the other one died as a by-product."

"Possible," Jesse said. "Any idea which was the target?"

"Well, certainly Walton was the most prominent," Hendricks said, "and after his death he was . . . displayed more prominently."

"Yes," Jesse said. "That's true. Anything else?"

No one spoke. Jesse smiled pleasantly at them.

"We will probably need to talk to each of you individually," Jesse said, "in the course of the investigation. We're not handy to each other, so it may take some travel. But we can phone and fax and e-mail. It's a small department, but we're very modern."

No one said anything. Jesse gave out his card to those who didn't have one.

"Detective Simpson, do you have anything to add?"

"No, sir," Suit said.

Jesse nodded and smiled at them all again.

"We'll be in touch," he said.

like those women," Suit said in the car driving north through Connecticut.

"In the carnal sense?" Jesse said.

"Of course not, I'm, like, almost a detective for crissake," Suit said. "I think if we push them a little, they will explode and a lot of stuff we don't know will come flying out."

"There's usually tension between ex- and current wives," Jesse said.

"You speaking from experience?" Suit said.

"Only way to speak," Jesse said.

"So what do you think about those people?" Suit said. "Seems to me they were all living off of Weeks and now he's gone, they're scrambling to see what's left."

"Why do you think so?" Jesse said.

"Couple of things. One: Of course anytime the milk cow dies everybody starts worrying about where they gonna get milk," Suit said.

Jesse nodded. The car went up the Charter Oak Bridge over the Connecticut River, with Hartford on the left.

"Second thing," Suit said. "Nobody seemed to be mourning the guy much."

"Sometimes after a murder," Jesse said, "people seem flat and without feelings. It's shock mostly."

"You know what kind of guy he was?" Suit said.

"No."

"Anyone say anything about him?" Suit said.

Jesse, from the passenger seat, glanced over at Suit and nodded slowly. Driving, his eyes on the road, Suit didn't see him nod.

"Not that I can remember, Detective Simpson," Jesse said.

"Nobody did," Suit said. "I went over my notes last night in the hotel. Nobody said they loved him. Nobody said the world lost a great man. Nobody said they'd miss him."

"Hendricks said he wanted to carry on Walton's legacy," Jesse said.

"What's that mean?" Suit said.

"I think it means he wants Weeks's job," Jesse said.

Suit nodded.

"And the wife, the current one," Suit said. "She didn't even claim the body."

Jesse nodded.

"And she didn't worry when he didn't come home, and she didn't even come up when she heard he was dead. Nobody came up. The lawyer, the manager, the researcher guy. I think we'll find that Lutz did all the arrangements."

"Hendricks," Jesse said.

"And the ex-wife," Suit said.

"Stephanie," Jesse said.

"That's why I take notes," Suit said. "I can't remember anybody's name."

"Whatever works. What about Stephanie."

"She implied that maybe the wife . . ."

"Lorrie."

"That Lorrie," Suit said, "might have been fooling around and didn't care if Weeks came home."

"She didn't quite say that," Jesse said.

"I think that's what she meant," Suit said.

"We'll see," Jesse said.

"We gonna stop up here in Vernon at that deli."

"Rein's," Jesse said. "Yeah, tongue sandwich on light rye."

"Tongue?"

"Yes."

"Cow tongue?"

"Uh-huh."

"Jesus," Suit said.

They turned off Route 84 at the proper entrance.

"Did I miss anything?" Suit said.

"In New York? No. Or if you did we both did," Jesse said.

"I don't think we did," Suit said.

"One suggestion, though," Jesse said. "Based on my years of experience."

"What?"

"The fact," Jesse said, "that you liked those women for evidence doesn't mean you couldn't also like them in the carnal sense."

"Wow," Suit said as he pulled the car into the parking lot in front of Rein's Deli. "No wonder you got to be chief."

"It's a gift," Jesse said.

**23**

How is it?" Jesse said to Sunny on the phone.

He sat with a drink at the bar in his living room, in front of his picture of Ozzie Smith.

"Better than I feared," Sunny said. "I was prepared to be sympathetic. We're both women and she was raped."

"The sisterhood is strong," Jesse said.

"You'll never understand," Sunny said.

"No," Jesse said.

He held the glass away from him and looked at the smooth whiskey and the clean ice. He drank some.

"But," Sunny said, "what I wasn't prepared for is . . . I like her."

"She's pretty likable," Jesse said.

"She is," Sunny said. "She's interested. She's smart. She listens. She gets it. She's funny. She's been around."

"I'll say."

"All of us have been around," Sunny said.

"I know."

"But for all of that, there's some quality in her," Sunny said, "that makes you want to protect her. Some sort of little-girl thing, like she really shouldn't be facing life alone."

"I know that, too," Jesse said.

He admired his whiskey.

"Yes. I can see why she's hard to let go of," Sunny said.

Jesse took another drink.

"Can I trust her?" Sunny said.

Jesse set the glass down on the counter.

"No," he said.

"Nobody's perfect," Sunny said.

"Some are less perfect than others," Jesse said. "Who's with her at night?'

"Nobody. She lives in a secure building. Twenty-four-hour concierge. I take her home when she's through for the night. And pick her up when she starts the morning."

"Doesn't leave a lot of time to find the rapist," Jesse said.

"If he's stalking her," Sunny said, "I'm hoping that maybe he'll find us."

"Is there a Plan B?"

"Of course there's a Plan B," Sunny said. "You remember my friend Spike."

"Yes."

"I'm going to introduce them," Sunny said, "and see if she'll let Spike babysit her sometimes, while I try to find the rapist."

"Spike would be effective," Jesse said. "She won't like it so much that he's gay."

"Because she can't vamp him?"

"Something like that," Jesse said.

"You know her," Sunny said.

"I know her better than anyone," Jesse said. He put some more ice into his glass as he talked, and added whiskey. "But I have no judgment about her. I know the facts of her, but I can't seem to make anything coherent out of what I know."

"Yes," Sunny said.

Jesse started on his second drink.

"How is Walton Weeks going?" Sunny said.

"Gathering information," Jesse said.

"Anything promising?"

"Too early."

"And the public attention doesn't help," Sunny said. "You're sitting there looking at this pile of unassociated data, and everyone is clamoring for an arrest."

"Clamoring," Jesse said. "He was a friend of the governor's."

"Oh God!" Sunny said.

"Uh-huh."

"We both know the first person to look at in a murder case," Sunny said.

"*Cherchez la* significant other?"

"*Oui.*"

"There's three ex-wives," Jesse said. "The current significant other got killed with him."

"Did she have a significant other," Sunny said, "besides Walton?"

"Good thought," Jesse said. "We don't know yet."

"You know what connection he had to Paradise?"

"Nope."

"You know his connection to the governor?" Sunny said.

"Nope."

"How about the bodyguard?" Sunny said.

"You've been following the case," Jesse said.

"I read the papers with interest," Sunny said. "I am tight with one of the cops involved."

"I suspected as much," Jesse said. "Bodyguard was a cop in Baltimore."

"You check that out?"

"Not yet," Jesse said. "If he were lying, why would he lie about something so easy to check?"

"Gun?"

"Carries a nine-millimeter Glock," Jesse said. "We test-fired it. It isn't the murder weapon."

"You'll find him," Sunny said. "Or her. Or them."

"Sometimes you don't," Jesse said.

"I know."

They were silent. Jesse thought he heard Sunny swallow.

"You having a drink?" he said.

"White wine," Sunny said. "Are you having scotch?"

"I am," Jesse said.

"Having a virtual drink together," Sunny said.

"Better than no drink at all," Jesse said.

They were quiet again. It was an easy quiet. There was no strain to it. There was never any strain between them, Jesse thought.

"Ever see Richie?" Jesse said.

"I saw him today," Sunny said. "He came to pick up Rosie for the weekend."

"She like that?"

"Yes. She's always happy to go with him."

"He still married?" Jesse said.

"Yes."

"Wife like Rosie?"

"Richie says so, and Rosie likes her."

"How's that feel?"

"Awful."

"You comfortable," Jesse said, "letting her go?"

"Yes. I miss her, but Richie would never let her be mistreated. He loves her as much as I do."

"How is it between you and Richie."

"When he's here?" Sunny thought about it. He heard her swallow. He took a drink. *Companionable.* "It's very difficult. For both of us. We are still so . . . so stuck together . . . it's hard to move naturally."

"He like that, too?" Jesse said.

Sunny thought about that.

"Richie is so interior, it is hard to tell," Sunny said. "But I think so. I don't think I'm projecting it onto him."

"Well," Jesse said. "Aren't we in a fucking mess."

Sunny took another sip of wine. She swallowed slowly, and Jesse could hear her pour more wine, the bottle clinking against the rim of her glass.

"I guess," Sunny said finally, "if I had to be in a fucking mess, there's no one I'd rather be in a fucking mess with."

"Me too," Jesse said.

J esse sat with Molly in the squad room watching videotapes of Walton Weeks. Molly was taking notes. On the
screen, Weeks was interviewing a congressman.

"I am not, of course, an economist," the congressman
said.

"Thank God," Weeks said.

"But I have yet to hear a valid argument against what
used to be called trickle-down economics."

"The theory that if rich people have money to spend,
they'll spend it, and everyone will benefit," Weeks said.

"Yes, as a means of redistributing money, it is infinitely more efficient than having us give it to the government for redistribution," the congressman said.

"In the form of taxes," Weeks said.

"Yes. If taxes are lowered for people with money, they'll do something with it. They won't pile it in the cellar. They'll invest it and some broker will get a commission. They'll buy a car and some salesman will get a commission. They'll build an addition to their house and carpenters, plumbers, electricians, et cetera, will be hired. The economy will benefit. Workers will benefit."

"Makes sense to me," Weeks said. "What about nonworkers?"

"Nonworkers?"

"Small children," Weeks said. "Mothers of small children, elderly men, people who can't work?"

"No one wishes to abandon those people, but higher taxes, and bigger welfare payments, are not the answer."

"What is the answer," Weeks said.

"We need to create stable families," the congressman said. "Families with husbands and fathers to care for their children, their wives, their elderly parents."

"How do we do that?"

"Walton, I'm not here to talk about social engineering," the congressman said.

"Of course you are," Weeks said. "What do you think taxes are?"

"Too high," the congressman said, "is what I think taxes are."

Weeks smiled and looked into the camera.

"On that note, we'll take a break," he said. "Be right back."

Jesse clicked the screen dark. Molly looked at her notes. Jesse stood and walked down the room and looked out the back window at the public works parking lot.

"Pretty reasonable guy," Jesse said.

"He asks hard questions and follows them up," Molly said, still looking at her notes. "But he isn't abrasive. He seems, like, actually interested, like there's no *gotcha* going on, you know?"

"I like the one an hour or so ago, when some other guy was talking about creating stable families, and Walton says, 'So are you in favor of gay marriage?'"

"Yes. You know what's good," Molly said. "He didn't put words in his mouth. He didn't say, 'Aha! So you are in favor of gay marriage.' He just asked the honest question."

"No wonder people liked him."

"You never watched him?"

"I only watch ball games," Jesse said. "What do we know about him from watching his program all day?"

"He's nonpartisan," Molly said. "He challenged this guy about how to help impoverished people. He challenged some black activist a while back on welfare."

She looked at her notes again.

"'If it's so good,' he said, 'why are there so many fewer intact black families than there were fifty years ago?'"

"Is that true?" Jesse said.

"How the hell do I know," Molly said. "But you tend to believe him when he says things."

"So he's likable and believable, and essentially nonpartisan," Jesse said. "He seems in a genuine search for the truth."

"Yes."

"No wonder somebody wanted to kill him," Jesse said.

"We don't want a lot of that going on in public," Molly said.

"Be the end of politics as we know it," Jesse said.

"Amazing they let him on television," Molly said.

"I got a folder full of his columns that I'll read tonight," Jesse said. "But, cynicism aside, he doesn't seem like somebody who would be murdered and hung from a tree because of his, for lack of a better word, politics."

"Is that why we watched all this?" Molly said. "To find that out?"

"Good to know about your victim."

"There were two victims," Molly said.

"I know," Jesse said. "But she didn't leave us videotape. We get his killer, we'll get hers."

"The thing is," Molly said, "it's like we've got too much. Videotapes, newspaper columns, two victims, three ex-wives, bodyguard, researcher, lawyer, manager, and God knows who else."

"There's no such thing as too much," Jesse said.

"Except that it's sort of daunting," Molly said.

"It's just work," Jesse said.

"A dauntingly lot of work," Molly said.

Jesse smiled.

"We can work."

Molly closed her notebook.

"*We* certainly can," Molly said. "My kids are starting to call me Aunt Mommy."

"Take tonight off," Jesse said.

"Omigod," Molly said. "Tough on the outside, tender on the inside."

"Probably the right arrangement," Jesse said. "For a cop."

Molly smiled.

"Sometimes you're the other way," Molly said.

"There's something I've been wondering about, Moll," Jesse said. "Maybe you can help me with it."

"Come into my parlor, said the spider to the fly."

"What," Jesse said.

"'Maybe you can help me' is usually code for 'Molly, there's something needs to be done that I don't want to do.'"

"Molly," Jesse said, "I'm the chief of police. I don't do, I delegate."

Molly nodded.

"And wonderfully well," she said. "What do you need?"

"As far as we know," Jesse said, "Weeks wasn't in the military. He wasn't licensed to carry a gun. He didn't have a security clearance."

"So?"

"So why do we have Walton Weeks's fingerprints in the system," he said.

Molly was silent for a moment.

Then she said, "I'll look into it, Chief."

Sunny and Spike drove Jenn home to her new condo at One Charles Street. Sunny sat with the motor idling while Spike took Jenn to her apartment and went in with her to make sure she was alone. It was early evening, a cold rain was falling, and the wind was strong. Across Charles Street, a man in a trench coat stood in the shelter of a doorway, his hands in his pockets, a wide-brimmed felt hat pulled down. Sunny studied him. There was no way to see his face. He didn't move. He could be the guy she'd seen outside King's Chapel. Or he could be Humphrey Bogart. Spike came back from Jenn's apartment and got in the front seat. On the floor,

Rosie raised her head and looked at Spike with some annoyance before she settled back down with her head against the heater.

"Dog's very territorial," Spike said.

"She needs her space," Sunny said.

"Dog weighs thirty pounds," Spike said. "I weigh about two-fifty. I need a little space myself."

"You wish you weighed two-fifty," Sunny said. "See that guy across the street?"

"Sort of," Spike said.

"I'm going to circle the block, see what he does when we're gone."

"You recognize him?" Spike said.

"I can't see him well enough."

"Want me to go ask him about himself?" Spike said.

"God, you're aggressive," Sunny said. "'Excuse me, sir, are you by any chance stalking someone?'"

"Just a thought," Spike said.

Sunny put the car in drive and headed toward Park Square. She turned left behind the Four Seasons hotel and left on Arlington and circled briefly through the South End and back onto Charles. The man was gone. Sunny continued on Charles slowly, but he wasn't in sight. Sunny went once again around the block. Again, nothing.

"Want a drink?" Sunny said.

"What about Rosie?" Spike said.

"We'll go to the Four Seasons," Sunny said. "Guys on the door will look out for her."

They sat at the bar downstairs. Sunny ordered a cosmopolitan. Spike had bourbon.

"So what do you think of Jenn?" Sunny said.

"I think I'm the perfect bodyguard for her."

"A tough fairy," Sunny said.

"I can protect her, and she can't seduce me."

"You think she would?"

"It's what she knows how to do," Spike said. "I don't know if she'd want sex or not, but she'd use it to get what she wanted. If I was straight, I'd follow her around like a beagle."

"She has a lot of juice."

"And she generates a lot of heat," Spike said.

"Spike, I didn't think you noticed things like that."

"I notice," Spike said. "I just don't care."

"Jesse said she wouldn't like you because she couldn't use her sex on you."

"Jesse's right," Spike said. "I think she'll accept me. I'm big and strong, and she's scared. But I know women like Jenn. She's not homophobic. My sex life is fine with her. But they only know how to relate to men in a sexual context, and when that's not available, as it's not with me, it makes them ill at ease."

"Some women like that."

"Yes, many. They are comfortable with a guy who's got no interest in seeing them naked. Jenn isn't one of them. She counts on men wanting to see her naked."

"You think she's promiscuous?"

Spike sipped some bourbon.

"Honey," he said, "I don't even know what promiscuous means anymore, except I'm probably in favor of it. I think she likes sex and will sleep with someone because she does."

"Nothing much wrong with that," Sunny said.

"You should know," Spike said. "But I don't think she's ever, what, driven by sex. She can have sex or not. But she never takes her eye off the prize."

"Which you think is more than a good time?" Sunny said.

"Yes."

"You know what the prize would be?" Sunny said.

Spike sipped more bourbon and held it a moment in his mouth before he swallowed.

"No," he said. "I'm not sure she does. But it's not about achieving orgasm."

"You only spent about three hours with her so far," Sunny said. "You seem to know an awful lot."

"Three hours is a long time if you pay attention," Spike said.

"And you're smart," Sunny said.

"That too," Spike said. "Plus, she reminds me of someone."

"Me?"

"No," Spike said. "I'm not sure you know what the prize is, but you don't use sex to get it."

"Thank you."

"You're welcome."

"So who's she remind you of?"

"Me," Spike said.

Sunny sat back in her chair with her cosmopolitan half-raised to her lips.

"Well," she said finally, "the physical resemblance is striking."

Spike shrugged. Sunny finished raising her glass. She drank and put the glass back down.

"How would you like to be in love with Jenn?" she said.

Spike shook his head slowly.

"Oh, Mama!" he said.

**26**

Suit came into Jesse's office and sat down.

"Molly said you wanted me to run down Weeks's fingerprints," he said.

Jesse smiled.

"She'll be chief someday," Jesse said.

"What?" Suit said.

Jesse shook his head.

"What have you got?" he said.

Suit took out his notebook.

"Walton Weeks was booked for public indecency in White Marsh, Maryland, in 1987."

"And fingerprinted at the time," Jesse said.

"That's what it says."

"Who booked him?"

"Baltimore County police."

"Got a name?" Jesse said.

"No."

"Phone?"

"Molly just said to find out why he was in the system," Suit said. "Is this going to delay my promotion to detective?"

"Probably," Jesse said and leaned forward and pulled the phone to him.

"You going to pursue the investigation yourself?" Suit said.

"I like to keep my hand in," Jesse said and dialed 411.

It took two holds and one second phone call before Jesse was talking to the sergeant in charge of Precinct 9 of the Baltimore County Police Department in White Marsh.

"We busted Walton Weeks," the sergeant said.

"Nineteen eighty-seven," Jesse said, "public indecency."

"For crissake," the sergeant said, "what'd he do, wave his willy at somebody?"

"I don't know," Jesse said. "I thought I'd ask you."

"Oh, oh," the sergeant said. "A test of our record-keeping."

"Anything you got," Jesse said.

"Where'd you say you were from?"

"Paradise, Massachusetts," Jesse said.

"Outside of Boston, right? Where Weeks got popped."

"You read the papers," Jesse said.

"And watch TV and listen to the radio," the cop said. "Good luck to you guys."

"Thanks."

There was silence. Jesse could hear the computer keys tapping.

"New system," the sergeant murmured.

"They're all new to me," Jesse said.

"Yeah," the sergeant said, "ain't that the truth." More tapping.

"Shit!" the sergeant said. His voice raised. "Alice, will you come over and run this goddamned thing for me."

Jesse heard a woman's voice murmur in the background.

"Walton Weeks," the sergeant said, "public indecency, 1987."

The woman's voice murmured again. The computer keys tapped. Jesse waited.

"Come on, come on, come on," the sergeant said.

Jesse knew he was talking to the computer.

"Okay," the sergeant said. "Here it is. Goddamn. Way to go, Walton."

"What," Jesse said.

"Got a couple of complaints at the White Marsh Mall. Officer went out and found Walton bopping some girl in the back of a Mercedes sedan."

"How old was the girl?"

"Bonnie Faison," the sergeant said. "Age nineteen."

"What was the disposition?"

"We booked them both, and that was the end of it. Case got dismissed pretty quick."

"Friends in high places," Jesse said.

"Well," the sergeant said, "it was a Mickey Mouse charge anyway. Damn arresting officer should have just shooed them away."

"Once he brought them in . . ."

"We had to book them."

"You know anything about the girl?" Jesse said.

"All I got is her address in 1987."

"I'll take it," Jesse said.

Molly came into Jesse's office with a woman. The woman wore a white tunic and black pants. Her black boots had three-inch heels. Her hair was black with a dramatic silver streak in the front. Jesse could sense Molly's approval in the way she ushered the woman in.

"Ellen Migliore," Molly said. "Chief Stone."

Jesse stood. They shook hands. The woman sat down. Molly left the door open and departed.

"The first Mrs. Walton Weeks," Jesse said.

"Yes," the woman said. "I'm sorry I didn't get here sooner. I live in Italy and I only recently heard about Walton."

"I'm sorry for your loss, Mrs. Migliore," Jesse said.

"Ellen, please," she said. "I have been away from Walton too long for this to be painful. But I was married to him for five years and I liked him."

Jesse nodded.

"What can I do for you, Ellen?"

"No, Chief, it's what can I do for you?"

"Jesse," he said. "That's why you came here? From Italy?"

"Yes," she said. "Genoa."

"Do you have anything specific?" Jesse said.

"No," she said. "I knew Walton a long time ago. But I knew him well, and I care. Are there funeral arrangements yet?"

Jesse nodded.

"Lorrie?"

"Yes, as soon as the ME released the body. It was a quick and private ceremony."

"ME?" she said.

"Medical examiner," Jesse said.

Ellen Migliore nodded and dropped her head for a moment and was silent.

Then she said, "Poor Walton."

Jesse nodded.

"So alone," Ellen said.

Jesse nodded.

"He was always so alone," Ellen said.

"Always?"

"Probably always. Certainly when I knew him."

"Even when he was with you?" Jesse said.

"With anyone and everyone," Ellen said.

"Talk about that," Jesse said.

He was back in his chair now, perfectly still, one foot propped, hands folded. Rain misted on the window behind him. In the month of May there had been five clear days.

"It was as if he knew a secret," she said. "A sad secret that only he knew, and it kept him a little separate from everyone. He was somehow distant, even in the most intimate of moments, even with the most intimate of companions."

"Like you," Jesse said.

"Like me, like every other woman, like every other person."

"What was the secret?"

"I don't know. I didn't even know how to ask him. He would have said there was no secret, that he wasn't distant."

"Maybe he would have been right," Jesse said.

"No," Ellen said. "He was distant. There was a silent space around him."

"Maybe he was just an interior guy," Jesse said.

"Like you," she said.

"Me?"

"Yes. You are very interior, and there is a shield of silence around you, too."

"But do I have a sad secret?"

"I don't know you well enough," Ellen said. "But if I slept with you for five years, I would know."

Jesse smiled.

"Not the worst idea I ever heard," Jesse said.

"I am too old for you," Ellen said.

"No," Jesse said. "You're not."

Ellen smiled and bowed her head slightly toward Jesse in acknowledgment.

"I always thought it was connected to the womanizing," she said.

"Womanizing," Jesse said.

"Yes. He was compulsive," she said.

"You think he did it because of his, ah, secret?" Jesse said. "Or that it was his secret?"

"I don't know," she said. "What I do know is that no matter how many women he had, his aloneness remained visceral."

"He was arrested outside Baltimore," Jesse said. "In 1987, for public indecency."

Ellen smiled sadly.

"No doubt with a young woman," she said.

"Yes. In the backseat of a car in the parking lot of a shopping mall."

"He liked young women," Ellen said.

"How young did he like them?" Jesse said.

"Sometimes maybe too young," Ellen said. "I don't know. If that's the only time he was caught, he's very lucky."

"Girl was Bonnie Faison, she was nineteen," Jesse said. "Mean anything to you?"

"No. But I wasn't with him by then. He was Stephanie's problem in 1987."

"Did he fool around when he was with you."

123

"Jesse," she said. "He could no more not fool around than he could not breathe. I don't think it was really a choice for him."

"So you assume he fooled around when he was with Stephanie?"

"Of course."

"And Lorrie?"

"Of course."

"Do you know Carey Longley?" Jesse said.

"The woman who died with him?"

"Yes."

"No, but I can describe her. Quite young. Quite pretty. Quite amazed to be with a man like Walton."

"She was young and pretty," Jesse said.

"I've known a hundred of her," Ellen said.

"She was also ten weeks pregnant," Jesse said.

Ellen sat silently for a moment.

"With Walton's child?"

"Yes."

"Oh," Ellen said, "my God."

Jesse waited. As he watched, Ellen Migliore teared up.

"How awful," she said. "To come so close, to finally come so close . . ."

"He wanted children?"

"Terribly," she said. "At least during our time."

"And you never had any."

"No," she said.

"Do you know why?"

"No," she said. "We never sought medical advice. I guess we were each more comfortable assuming the other one was at fault."

"Have you had any since?"

"Three," she said.

"So you figured it was his, ah, fault," Jesse said.

"I know, fault isn't the right word, and by the time I was having my children, I wasn't really thinking much about Walton—but yes, one would have assumed that he was the infertile one in our marriage."

"Apparently neither of you were," Jesse said.

"He never had children in either of his other marriages," Ellen said.

"Maybe this time he got medical help."

"That would not be the Walton Weeks I knew," Ellen said.

"People change," Jesse said.

"Not without help," Ellen said.

"Psychiatric help?"

"Yes. And Walton would never consider it."

Jesse smiled.

"Sometimes people change," he said.

Ellen shrugged slightly.

"Or circumstances do," she said.

"You think he needed shrink help," Jesse said.

"The infertility thing bothered him," she said. "And that distance-around-him thing, and . . . the womanizing. Yes, he needed help."

"Do you know the other wives?" Jesse said.

"I've met them. I don't really know them."

"Do you know why he was in Boston?"

"No."

"Do you know of any connection with Paradise."

"Of course," she said. "You don't know?"

Jesse shook his head.

"He used to come here as a boy. His parents would rent a place every summer. He and his mother would spend the summers here. His father would come on the weekends."

"Where was the house?" Jesse said.

"He said it was near the beach. Some college professor went to Europe every summer and rented his house out."

"Did he ever come here later?" Jesse said.

"Not that I know of. But it was always, pardon the pun, a paradise lost for him. He always talked about it as if it were magical."

"Do you have any idea who might have killed him?"

"No," she said.

Jesse was quiet.

"But," she said, "I'll bet it was a woman, or about a woman."

"Do you have an alibi for the time of his death?" Jesse said.

"I know you have to ask," she said. "Yes, I have an alibi."

"I haven't told you exactly when he died," Jesse said.

"It doesn't matter," Ellen Migliore said. "I haven't left Italy in five years."

"And you can prove it," Jesse said.

"Yes."

"That should cover you," Jesse said. "Do you have time to give us a statement today?"

"Of course," she said. "Will there be any kind of memorial service for Walton?"

"Not that I know of," Jesse said.

"How sad. Shuffled off the stage so quickly, and with so few trumpets."

"He may not care," Jesse said.

Ellen nodded.

"I'll ask Molly Crane to take your statement," Jesse said.

"Police chiefs don't take statements?" she said.

"Police chiefs tend to screw up the tape recorder," Jesse said.

"I'm not so sure," Ellen said, "that I believe you've ever screwed up anything."

"Maybe a few relationships," Jesse said.

**28**

S ome people," Dix said, "find that they are infertile and are saddened but say, in effect, 'We still have each other,' and get on with their lives. Some adopt. Some fear infertility as a personal failure and refuse to be tested, or even admit to it. These people usually blame their partner."

The office walls were bare white. There was a green couch against one wall. Jesse had never been on it. Through the window Jesse could see the treetops tossing a bit in the wind, and the gray clouds being pushed aside by the same wind. There was some blue sky showing.

Dix smiled briefly.

"It is these people," he said, "whom we see most often."

"And their partners," Jesse said.

"Often," Dix said. "I am not enthusiastic about couples counseling. But in some cases it seems effective. If more intensive therapy seems indicated, I refer one of them."

"Is there anyone in Boston," Jesse said, "especially famous for dealing with such issues?"

"Jonah Levy," Dix said. "He's a psychiatrist, in practice with a gynecologist named Frances Malloy, who probably knows more about the biology of infertility than anyone in the world, and a urologist named Edward Margolis, who would know more about infertility than anyone in the world if it weren't for Frances."

"They'd be widely known?"

"Very."

"Nationally?"

"Worldwide," Dix said.

"So it's plausible that Walton Weeks might come up here to seek his help."

"It is quite plausible," Dix said. "Any fertility specialist in the world might well refer a difficult fertility case to Jonah. Particularly a high-profile one."

"Because?"

"High-profile?"

"Yes."

"Because Jonah is both very expensive and very discreet. One assumes Walton Weeks could afford him and would want discretion."

"Do you know them?" Jesse said.

"I know Jonah."

"If he was treating Weeks, and maybe Carey Longley, would he talk about it? Privileged communication and all?"

"Most doctors are guided by their patients' best interests," Dix said. "It would seem that Weeks's best interest, and Longley's, if she was a patient as well, would be served by talking about it."

"Inasmuch as it might help solve their murder," Jesse said.

"Inasmuch," Dix said.

"That sounds pretty sensible," Jesse said.

"Don't believe that all-shrinks-are-crazy myth," Dix said.

"Would a man who had unresolved emotional issues about fertility be likely to be a womanizer?" Jesse said.

"Such a man might keep looking for the woman who could conceive for him," Dix said. "Or he might avoid women because he didn't want to once again face his own failure."

"Weeks was a womanizer."

"Or he enjoyed sex," Dix said. "Sometimes a cigar is just a cigar."

"If his first wife is correct, it was obsessive."

"If so, maybe it was the fertility issue. Maybe he hated women. Maybe he loved them. Maybe he was trying to re-create the relationship with his mother. Maybe he was asserting his manhood for reasons unrelated to fertility. Maybe he was avenging himself on a wife. Maybe it was an interactive cluster of those things, or things we don't even imagine."

"Do I hear you saying we don't know why Weeks was a womanizer?" Jesse said.

"You do," Dix said. "Like many shrinks, I do better with one patient at a time with whom I have regularly spent time."

"How disappointing," Jesse said.

"Think how I feel," Dix said.

29

Y ou're back," Jesse said when Suitcase Simpson came into his office.

"Been eating a lot of crab cakes," Suit said.

"They do that in Baltimore. Drink a little National Bo with the crab cakes?"

"Only while off duty," Suit said.

He saluted with three fingers, like a Boy Scout. Jesse thought Suit seemed very pleased with himself.

"Do anything else?" Jesse said.

"I found Bonnie Faison," Suit said.

"Really?" Jesse said.

"Yep. Wasn't easy. But for a man with my crime detection instincts . . ."

"Was she still at the last address they had for her?" Jesse said.

"Yep. That Baltimore County cop went over with me."

"Sergeant Franks," Jesse said.

"Yeah, him," Suit said. "She's at the same place. She's almost forty, got two kids and no husband, lives with her mother."

"Sounds great," Jesse said.

"Yeah. I don't think anyone's happy about it," Suit said. "But there they are. Three-bedroom ranch, yard about the size of a pool table. Some sort of inbred dog looks like a hyena."

"She remember the incident?"

"After a while," Suit said. "She didn't want to talk about it, but Franks sort of convinced her she had to or else."

Jesse nodded.

"Tell you one thing," Suit said. "I hope she looked better when Weeks was poking her."

Jesse nodded again.

"Man, she's so fat, I don't think you'd know if you were in," Suit said.

"Maybe she was better at nineteen," Jesse said.

"I hope so."

"How'd she meet Weeks?" Jesse said.

"She was hanging out at the mall, and picked him up after a book signing."

"She the aggressor?" Jesse said.

"Sounds that way. Her mother said she just wanted to fuck a celebrity."

"Maternal pride," Jesse said.

"Her mother says she woulda fucked anybody she saw on television, before she got too fat."

"You're quoting," Jesse said.

"Uh-huh," Suit said. "Mother's skinny as a lizard. Smoked about two packs of cigarettes while we were there."

"Bonnie ever see Weeks again?"

"No. He gave her his phone number, but when she called it she found out it was some restaurant in Baltimore."

"So she never saw him again."

"Nope," Suit said, "but they'll always have the White Marsh Mall."

He went to the coffeemaker on top of Jesse's file cabinet and poured some coffee, added sugar and nondairy creamer, and took a sip.

"How old were the kids," Jesse said.

"Little kids, you know, eight, ten years old, maybe. I don't know much about kids."

Suit drank some coffee.

"Anything else?" Jesse said.

"Well, yeah, a little something," Suit said.

Jesse waited. Suit drank another swallow of coffee.

"On the ride back to the station," Suit said, "Franks and I were, you know, talking, and I asked him what happened to the arresting officer, you know, the guy busted Weeks. And Franks says he was around for a while, made detective, and then quit. Went into private security. So I say, for nothing, what was his name?"

"Lutz," Jesse said.

"You knew?"

Jesse smiled.

"No," Jesse said, "but the way you were ready to wet yourself telling me, who else was it going to be? Rumpelstiltskin?"

"Man, you know how to ruin stuff," Suit said.

"So you followed up," Jesse said. "And it's our Lutz."

"Yes. Conrad Lutz," Suit said. "Be some kind of coincidence if it was a different Conrad Lutz."

"If it came to that, we could fingerprint him," Jesse said. "He'd be on file."

"So whaddya make of that, Jesse?"

"Good police work by you, sloppy by me," Jesse said. "I should have asked when I called them."

"Does this mean a salary increase for me?"

"No."

"Even if it turns out I've cracked the case?" Suit said

"Puts you right at the top of the list for detective."

"Soon as we have detectives," Suit said.

"Right after that," Jesse said.

Suit shrugged.

"It means Lutz lied to us," he said.

"Or at least left stuff out," Jesse said.

"We maybe should ask him about that?" Suit said.

"Sooner or later," Jesse said.

"First, you want to get all your ducks in a row?"

"I'd settle for getting them herded into the same area," Jesse said.

30

Jesse stood with Sunny Randall, leaning on the railing at the town wharf, looking down at the dark water. The day was overcast again, and the wind off the water was cooler than it should have been in May. Jesse was very aware that their shoulders touched. On her leash, Rosie sat at Sunny's feet in her bull-terrier sit, with her rear feet splayed and her tongue out. She too appeared to be interested in the harbor.

"Where's Jenn," Jesse said.

"Spike's with her," Sunny said.

"They get along?" Jesse said.

"Sort of. Jenn seems sort of uneasy with him. But it's hard not to like Spike."

"You getting along?"

Sunny nodded.

"Yes," she said. "And no, we haven't talked about you."

"Thought never entered," Jesse said. "Making any progress on who did it?"

"That's why I wanted to talk," Sunny said. "Right after I started taking care of her, we were eating lunch and I spotted a guy who seemed to be watching us through the window. I pointed him out to Jenn, and she said no, that was not the man."

Jesse nodded. Rosie spotted a seagull and stiffened, motionless, looking at it. The seagull went about his business.

"But the thing is," Sunny said, "I've seen him twice again. The last time I saw him I tried her again and she said no, and didn't seem to remember that I'd pointed him out before."

Jesse stared for a while at the water moving against the stone base of the wharf. Then slowly he raised his eyes and looked across the harbor at the neck. It was still morning, and the strength of the sun out of the east made him squint even through the overcast.

"Shit," he said after a time.

"Yes," Sunny said.

Jesse looked up at the overcast, and rolled his neck as if to stretch out a cramp.

"Well, at least someone's actually following her," he said.

"Yes."

Rosie held the seagull in her laser-like stare. The seagull had flown up on a pier piling and was staring back at Rosie.

"You ever notice that Rosie and the seagull have similar eyes?" Jesse said.

"Beady?"

"I guess," Jesse said.

Sunny smiled.

"But soulful," she said.

"In Rosie's case," Jesse said.

"Exactly."

They were quiet. The seagull flew away. Rosie watched it briefly, then turned her blank attention to the harbor, where the gray water was calm and the upright masts of the sailboats were nearly still.

"This Walton Weeks thing is burying me," Jesse said.

"I know. It's okay. I'll take care of Jenn."

"We need to know if she actually was raped."

"I know."

"I can't get away from the Weeks thing."

"I'll find out about the rape," Sunny said.

"Could the stalker be someone different than the rapist?" Jesse said.

"Seems crazy," Sunny said.

"Why would she refuse to ID him if he was the rapist?"

Sunny was looking at the harbor, too.

"Don't know," she said.

"Didn't she tell us the rapist was stalking her?"

"She told you that," Sunny said.

"And she told me she didn't know him before the rape."

"Yes."

"But that she recognized him as the rapist when he was stalking her."

"Yes," Sunny said.

"Any sign of anyone else stalking her?"

"No."

"You have a plan?" Jesse said.

"Spike and I have been discussing one," Sunny said.

"We want her safe," Jesse said. "But we want him for the rape, too."

"I know. If Spike had a talk with him, I'm sure he'd stop with the stalking. But, like you, I don't want to scare him away. I want to know what's going on."

"Maybe you could get them in a room together," Jesse said.

"That's what Spike and I are talking about."

"And?" Jesse said.

"I need to know she can do it. That it won't traumatize her worse than she already has been."

"If she was traumatized at all," Jesse said.

"Something happened," Sunny said. "I may not know her like you do . . . but something happened."

"Yes," Jesse said. "I think so, too."

At the open end of the harbor, a lobster boat plodded in around the outer tip of Stiles Island.

"She asked me to get her a gun," Jesse said.

"I have several," Sunny said.

Jesse nodded.

"You can issue her the license."

Jesse nodded again.

"But," Sunny said, "you're not sure she should be walking around with a gun."

"No," Jesse said. "I'm not."

"It should be her call, Jesse."

"She doesn't even know how to shoot," Jesse said.

"I can teach her."

"You think she should have one?" Jesse said.

"Believe her story for a moment," Sunny said. "Think about what that might be like. Would you like to face an overpowering enemy with no gun?"

Jesse nodded. The lobster boat had rounded Stiles Island now and was moving stolidly along the shoreline of Paradise Neck.

"And if we don't believe her story?" Jesse said.

"Something has happened to her," Sunny said. "She feels she needs a gun."

"And maybe she needs to be trusted."

"Skeptically," Sunny said.

"We think we might want to be together, you and I," Jesse said.

"And here we are worrying about one of the people who may keep us from being together," Sunny said.

"It's hard work," Jesse said.

"But we need to do it," Sunny said.

Jesse looked at her. He felt the pull of her. But it was not the same kind of pull Jenn exerted. Nothing was. There was no other feeling like the one Jenn caused. *Obsessions are fearsome.*

"Okay," Jesse said. "Give her a gun."

Sunny smiled.

"I already did," she said.

31

Healy pushed through the crowd of reporters outside the Paradise police station.

A reporter held out his microphone and said, "Who are you, sir?"

"The Pied Piper," Healy said. "When I leave, I want you all to follow me out of town."

He went in through the front door and closed it behind him.

At the desk Molly said, "Hi, Captain."

"Hello, darling," Healy said.

"Officer Darling," Molly said. "Chief Stone is in his office."

Healy grinned at her and went down the hall. In Jesse's office he went straight to the file cabinet and got some coffee. Then he sat down and crossed his legs.

"Thought I'd stop by," Healy said, "on my way to work, see how fame was affecting you."

"I think I'm opposed to freedom of the press."

"King Nixon might have agreed," Healy said.

"Okay," Jesse said. "It has its place."

"Just not here," Healy said.

"Exactly."

"You know anything I don't know?" Healy said.

"Probably," Jesse said. "But not about Walton Weeks."

"How 'bout Carey Longley?"

"Less," Jesse said.

"She's thirty years old, from New Jersey. Her father's an executive with Curtiss-Wright," Healy said. "Her mother's a housewife. Two older brothers, both work at Curtiss-Wright. She was married to and divorced from a guy who works for her father."

"So how come nobody has contacted me?" Jesse said.

"They all disowned her," Healy said. "They're very religious. When she divorced their handpicked husband and went off to work for Walton Weeks, and live sinfully, they all agreed she was no more."

"They don't like Walton?" Jesse said.

"They felt him to be an embodiment, I believe the phrase was, of the Antichrist," Healy said.

"Gee," Jesse said. "He didn't seem so bad, watching him on tape."

"That's because you're not as, ah, Christian as they are."

"Probably not," Jesse said. "What's your source?"

"Jersey state cop," Healy said. "Named Morrissey. Want to talk with him?"

"Maybe," Jesse said. "She have children?"

"No."

"Is Longley her maiden name or married name?"

"Married."

"What was her maiden name?" Jesse said.

"Young, and I think you're supposed to call it her birth name."

"Sure," Jesse said. "Her ex-husband disown her, too?"

"Yep."

"Everybody—father, mother, brothers, ex-husband."

"Sinful is sinful," Healy said.

"I wonder if one of them killed him for embodying the Antichrist, and her for carrying his baby."

"And they shot them instead of stoning them to death?" Healy said.

"Just a thought," Jesse said.

"It's not a bad one," Healy said. "Except according to Morrissey they all had alibis for the time she died."

"So does everyone else," Jesse said.

"Ex-wives?" Healy said.

"Yep. And the researcher and the manager and the lawyer."

"How about his bodyguard?" Healy said.

"Lutz? The day the ME says they died, the house dick at the hotel says Lutz had breakfast in the dining room, hung in the lobby all morning with a newspaper. He ate lunch in the dining room. Sat in the lobby, chatted up the doorman, used the health club, had a couple drinks in the bar, ordered room service for dinner and a movie and made two phone calls. He never left the hotel."

"Sounds like he wanted to be able to prove he was there," Healy said.

"It does," Jesse said. "And he was."

Healy nodded. Jesse turned the coffee mug slowly in his hands. Healy was neat and quiet in the chair across from him. Tan summer suit, blue shirt, tan tie with diagonal blue stripes, snap-brimmed summer straw hat with a big blue band.

"Two people murdered," Jesse said. "One of them famous. And no one appears to care at all."

"Except the first wife," Healy said.

Jesse nodded and looked out the window at the transmitter trucks parked near the station.

"And the Fourth Estate," he said.

"I don't think they care about Carey and Walton," Healy said.

"No," Jesse said. "Of course they don't. They're just subject matter."

Healy nodded.

"Ellen Migliore," Jesse said. "Who's divorced from Walton twenty years or more. She's the only one."

"I wonder why she cares?" Healy said.

"Something ulterior?" Jesse said.

"Doesn't hurt to think about it," Healy said.

"No," Jesse said. "It doesn't."

"Except then it leaves nobody who cares," Healy said.

Jesse looked at his coffee cup for a moment. Then he looked up at Healy.

"You and me," Jesse said. "We care."

"We're supposed to," Healy said.

J onah Levy held his office door for Jesse and waited until Jesse was seated before closing it and going to his own desk.

"Dix called me," Dr. Levy said, "on your behalf."

"Good," Jesse said.

"He says you are a very smart man."

"He would know," Jesse said.

"How can I help you?"

"Did you treat Walton Weeks?" Jesse said.

"Myself and my colleagues."

"For infertility?"

"Yes."

"Successfully," Jesse said.

"I gather that he had fathered a child before his death," Levy said.

"Yes. With Carey Longley."

"We worked with her as well," Levy said.

He was a small man in a gray suit and white shirt. His hair was receding. His glasses had gold rims. His tie was flamboyantly red and gold.

"What was the problem," Jesse said.

Levy examined one of his thumbnails for a moment.

"Mr. Weeks rarely ejaculated," Levy said.

"He was impotent?"

"No. He had no trouble erecting. He had trouble ejaculating."

"So," Jesse said. "He could do the deed, but he couldn't, ah, finish it off."

Levy smiled.

"One could put it that way," he said.

"Did he ever?" Jesse said.

"Infrequently. Too infrequently, it seems, to give him much chance of engendering a child."

"That's it?" Jesse said. "Just that? No biomechanical obstruction, no physical dysfunction, just didn't finish?"

"Just didn't finish," Levy said. "Had it been something physical, it might well have been easier to fix."

"Why?" Jesse said.

"Why didn't he, ah, finish?"

"Yes."

Levy leaned back, clasped his hands behind his head, and smiled at Jesse.

"How much time do you have?" Levy said.

"I don't need to be board-certified," Jesse said. "A concise summary would work."

Levy closed his eyes and pursed his lips and tilted his head back and thought for a moment.

Then he said, "You are, I assume, familiar with ambivalence."

Jesse smiled.

"My old friend," he said.

"Weeks wanted a child," Levy said. "And desperately did not want to share it with a woman."

"That's it?"

"There's never an *it*," Levy said. "There are always several *its*. There were issues of power—if he could arouse a woman sexually, he had power. If she could cause him to ejaculate, she had power. There was rage against all the women who had failed to give him full sexual release."

"Whom he punished by not achieving full sexual release," Jesse said.

"And punished him by denying him what he wanted."

Jesse whistled softly.

"Craziness has a nice symmetry, doesn't it," Jesse said.

"Often," Levy said.

"Can we say concisely why he was like this?"

"Not really," Levy said. "No surprise—it had to do with his mother and his childhood encounters with women. Certainly his mother sexualized their relationship."

"She molest him?"

"In the conventional way?" Levy said. "Probably not. But because of the inappropriate nature of their relationship, sex became the ultimate expression of love and, because it was his mother, horribly frightening. And it remained so, lodged there in his unconscious, all his life."

"So what happened?" Jesse said.

"To bring him here?"

"Yeah. He's fifty, he's had three wives, a million women, no kids. What made him come to you all of a sudden?"

Levy looked at his thumbnail again. He didn't answer. Jesse waited. Finally Levy looked up at Jesse.

"I don't know."

"Wow," Jesse said.

Levy smiled.

"We don't like to say that much."

"I say it all the time," Jesse said.

"I'm saying it more often," Levy said, "than I used to. Clearly, it had to do with the woman."

"Carey Longley," Jesse said.

"Yes."

"He wanted to have a baby with her."

"Yes," Levy said. "They talked of buying a home together."

"Where?" Jesse said.

"In Paradise," Levy said. "Unless they were being meta-phorical."

"What about his current wife?"

"It is my impression he had given her no thought. He was entirely consumed with this relationship."

"Ain't love grand," Jesse said.

Levy smiled. The two men sat quietly for a moment.

"What do you think about love, Doctor?" Jesse said.

"I remain agnostic about love," Levy said. "But there is clearly a connection between . . . there clearly was a connection between them that seemed to have been lacking in other instances."

"What made her special?"

"I don't know," Levy said.

"Did he have an explanation?"

"He simply said that he loved her, and had never loved anyone else."

"You talk with her?"

"Yes."

"She deserve it?" Jesse said.

"I don't know that deserve is an issue in these kinds of situations," Levy said. "She seemed to reciprocate."

"So it wasn't because she was, for lack of a better word, better than all the others?"

Levy looked at Jesse for a moment.

"No, often in these matters, flaws are the appeal."

"How about in this case?"

"I don't know," Levy said.

"But if you weren't agnostic about it, you could probably say that we love who we love whether we should or not, even though there are more suitable people to love."

"Are we still talking about Mr. Weeks?" Levy said.

Jesse was silent for a moment. He could feel his heartbeat; he was aware of his own breathing. Then he smiled at Levy.

"No," Jesse said. "We're not."

I t was a little after noon. Jesse and Suit were having sandwiches and coffee at Daisy's Restaurant. Daisy herself was
being interviewed by a woman in front of a television camera.

"Still news?" Jesse said to the waitress.

"Now it's follow-up," the waitress said. "You know, how
has the discovery of a body in your Dumpster affected your
business and your life."

"I thought Daisy hated the press," Suit said.

"I guess she don't," the waitress said. "We got rhubarb pie
for dessert. You want me to save you some."

"Please," Jesse said.

"The poor bastard," Suit said.

"Weeks?"

"Yeah, he finally finds the girl of his dreams and she's finally pregnant and somebody comes along and dumps them both."

Jesse nodded.

"Might be a connection," Jesse said.

"Maybe the wife?" Suit said. "Jealous?"

"Maybe," Jesse said.

They ate for a moment in silence, watching Daisy talk to the reporter on camera.

"You know the one thing is bothering me?" Jesse said.

"Just one?" Suit said.

"One of many," Jesse said. "They, together, had an appointment with Dr. Levy two weeks before they were killed. And they didn't show up."

"No cancellation?"

"No. Just never appeared. Levy's office called them and no one answered."

"Where'd they call?" Suit said.

"Hotel," Jesse said.

"Here? In Boston?"

"Yeah, the Langham."

"Except for the time," Suit said, "you'd think that was because they were dead."

"You would," Jesse said.

"Except the ME says it was only a few days before we found them," Suit said.

"Depending on the body's environment," Jesse said.

"You mean somebody maybe tried to fool us?"

"I don't mean anything, Suit. I'm grabbing at every straw that floats past. I want to know how long they were at the Langham. I want to know when they were last seen."

"Didn't Lutz say he'd seen them last walking up Franklin Street," Suit said.

"He said the doorman had seen them walking up Franklin Street," Jesse said. "And, you know, he never exactly said when that was."

"I could ask him," Suit said.

"Let's just keep track of him for now," Jesse said, "while I give it all some thought."

"We could have some pie," Suit said, "while you were doing that."

"I'll need the energy," Jesse said.

34

Jesse sat on the edge of Marcy Campbell's desk while she ran through her files.

"It is a booming real-estate market," Marcy said. "I have sold more houses already this year than I sold all of last."

She picked up a sheet of paper, glanced at it, put it back in the folder.

"I keep track of everything bought and sold in the last twelve months," she said.

"Sold by you?" Jesse said.

"Sold by anyone," Marcy said. "I like to keep track."

"How's your love life?" Jesse said.

"Busy, but we could always share a moment," Marcy said. "Where are you with Jenn?"

"I don't know."

"You're still serious about her," Marcy said.

"I am, and another woman as well."

"And you're serious about her."

"Yes."

"Which are you more serious about?" Marcy said.

"I don't know."

She put the folder away and took out another.

"Drinking?" Marcy said.

"Not bad, I'm drinking less than I'd like to."

"Don't we all," Marcy said. "Want me to lock the office and pull down the shade?"

Jesse smiled at her.

"Rain check?" he said.

"Of course," Marcy said. "What are friends for?"

"I think I know," Jesse said.

Marcy grinned.

"Seriousness not required," she said and shook her head. "No Walton Weeks."

"How about Carey Longley?"

While Marcy looked, Jesse walked to the front window of the small office and looked out at the narrow street that led to the harbor. The houses were close together. There were no yards. The front doors were separated from the street only by a narrow sidewalk. The street was too narrow to permit parking, and as Jesse stood there, no cars passed. Two hundred years ago it must have looked much the same.

"No Carey Longley," Marcy said. "I do have a Carey Young."

"Bingo," Jesse said without turning around. "Maiden name."

"They didn't want anyone to know," Marcy said.

"Trying to be private," Jesse said.

"And dying very publicly," Marcy said.

"Where's the property?"

"Stiles Island," Marcy said. "Outer side. Private beach, six rooms. Four-point-two million."

"For six rooms?"

"That's what it says."

"You sell it?" Jesse said.

"No. Ed Reamer, at Keyes Realty."

"Have an address for the house?" Jesse said.

"On the sheet," Marcy said.

She stood and walked to the window and stood beside Jesse and handed him the sheet. Then she leaned her head against his shoulder.

"Life's pretty hard," she said. "Isn't it."

"It is," Jesse said.

"Want a hug?" Marcy said.

"I do," he said.

**35**

I t was a one-story stone house with a cedar-shingled roof. The living room occupied the entire front, all glass facing the ocean. There was a big fireplace on the right-hand end wall with a raised hearth. The kitchen was green granite and stainless steel. There were two bedrooms, each with a full bath, and a room with a smaller fireplace, which was probably going to be a den. The house was empty. The flagstone floors gleamed with a new finish. The walls were newly painted. There was no furniture, no rugs, no drapes, no china, no crystal, no toothpaste, no towels, nothing to suggest human life. *Like seeing a person naked,* Jesse thought.

He stood in the silent living room and stared out past the patio, and across the small silver beach, at the gray Atlantic Ocean. Here along the North Shore, the ocean was cold, Jesse knew, even in the summer. It took fortitude to swim in it. Jesse walked the length of the room. There was no place in the room where you couldn't see the ocean.

*They would have put the dining area here,* Jesse thought. *Near the kitchen. And in the winter, they would have had a big fire in the fireplace and had drinks from the built-in wet bar, and watched the spray splatter against the thermopane during a storm. This would have been Walton's office. With the nice bay window looking at the ocean. This would have been the master bedroom, nice skylight. This one would have been the kid's room.* Jesse stood in the room feeling, suddenly, the thwarted reality of the ten-week fetus. He walked into the kitchen. *A big range hood over a built-in barbecue. A pantry off the rear wall, with a walk-in refrigerator. The dream house. Every convenience. The dream must have seemed so close. Reach out and take hold of it. All of it. Wife and child. At long last, love. A walk-in refrigerator!*

Jesse went in. The room was maybe eight by eight, with shelves along the three walls. There was nothing stored there. The shelves were empty. The compressor was shut off. The windowless room was warm. There was a thermostat on the wall. It was set to thirty-five. Jesse turned the switch on. Somewhere he could hear the compressor begin to run quietly. Soon he began to feel cold air. He walked around the empty space and saw nothing. He went back to the thermostat and shut it off and left the refrigeration room.

He stood for a time in the living room, listening to nothing, feeling the emptiness. Then he went outside and walked down to the beach and looked at the water. It was restless and active on the outer side of the island. There were whitecaps. The tide was high and there wasn't much beach above the reach of the waves. The way the coastline curved, there were no other houses in sight, and he couldn't see the road from where he stood.

He took his cell phone out of his pocket and dialed.

"Molly," he said. "I'm at Five Stiles Island Road. Send Peter Perkins out here with all his stuff. Tell him he's going to be looking for blood."

"Whose blood?" Molly said.

"I don't know yet."

"Has it to do with Walton Weeks?" Molly said.

"I don't know yet."

"But it might?" Molly said.

"Or it might not," Jesse send. "Could you see if you can find Peter Perkins."

"Yessir," Molly said.

**36**

Sunny had supper with Jenn at the Union Street Bar and Grill, in the South End, across from the cathedral. Several people recognized Jenn and pointed her out to companions. When they came out, Sunny saw the stalker lingering across the street, near the sheltered bus stop. Sunny paid him no attention. She patted her left thigh as if in time to music, and gave the valet her ticket. As she got into the car she glanced in her side-view mirror and saw Spike get out of his car, two blocks back on Washington Street. She smiled and when the valet closed the door for Jenn, she put the car in gear and drove away without looking back.

"I need to swing by my place," Sunny said, "before I drop you off."

Jenn nodded. She sat with her head back against the car seat and her eyes closed.

"What's your ex-husband like?" Jenn said.

Sunny thought about it.

"Richie's father and uncle run a mob," she said.

"They're gangsters?"

"Yes."

"How about him?"

"I'm not sure."

"You were married to him?" Jenn said. "You maybe still love him? And you're not sure?"

"I don't think Richie is even sure."

"Is he a criminal?" Jenn said.

"No," Sunny said. "I don't believe that he is. But he is very loyal to his father and his uncle."

"Even if it means being, ah, you know, illegal?"

"Yes."

"How do you feel about that?" Jenn said.

"It scares me," Sunny said.

She turned right off the northbound surface road and onto the Summer Street Bridge. Fort Point Channel was thick and dark beneath them.

"But," Sunny said, "I guess I understand. I'm quite close to my father."

"I envy you that," Jenn said.

"You don't have family, or you're not close?"

"Not close," Jenn said. "What is he like, Richie? I mean, to be with."

"He's nearly impervious," Sunny said. "Very contained. Quiet. But there's something going on in there. Something that you think might explode someday."

"At you?"

"No," Sunny said. "Not at me."

"Sounds a little like Jesse," Jenn said.

"Yes," Sunny said. "He is rather like Jesse."

"Jesse is so controlled, but you know that he has something very dangerous in there."

"Dangerous to you?" Sunny said.

Jenn opened her eyes and looked at Sunny and smiled.

"No," she said. "Not to me."

They parked on the street in front of Sunny's building.

"It's exciting, isn't it?" Sunny said.

"Exciting?" Jenn said.

"Yes, having that kind of power."

Jenn stared at her. The interior of the car was dimly lit by the street lamps. Sunny couldn't see Jenn's face very well.

"I never quite thought of it that way," Jenn said after a time. "But yes. To be with someone who is dangerous but would never be dangerous to you . . ."

"So why are we both divorced?" Sunny said.

"I don't know. I wish to God I did know. He's like the one necessity in my life. He's all I have for family. I know he loves me. I would trust him with my life."

"But?" Sunny said.

"But I can't stay with him. I can't be faithful to him. When I try I get claustrophobic."

"And you don't know why," Sunny said.

"No. Do you?"

"No," Sunny said. "We're working on it."

"We?"

"My shrink and I," Sunny said.

"Oh God," Jenn said. "I spend half my salary on shrinks."

"If at first you don't succeed," Sunny said.

They got out of the car and went into Sunny's building.

H ealy sat in Jesse's office with his hat on and one foot
against the edge of Jesse's desk.

"Okay," Healy said. "You were right. It's Weeks's blood
and the girl's."

"Carey Longley."

"Yes."

"So they were killed there," Jesse said. "Or somewhere,
and put in there, and kept cold."

"So we have no real idea when they were killed," Healy
said.

"Which means everybody's alibi is essentially meaningless," Jesse said.

"Which is probably why they were cold-stored in the first place," Healy said.

"Somebody knew what they were doing," Jesse said. "They just kept them cold and didn't freeze them. The ME would have been able to tell that they'd been frozen."

"Remember it sounded like Lutz was establishing an alibi sitting in the lobby and such."

Jesse nodded.

"How would he know when we'd decide they died?" Jesse said.

"He wouldn't," Healy said.

"So I guess he just likes to hang around hotels," Jesse said.

"I guess," Healy said.

"And I guess we'll have to reinterview everybody with the new understanding that we don't know when they died."

"Looks like," Healy said.

"Might dig them up," Jesse said.

"Might. If the Weeks estate would let you."

"Or we got a court order," Jesse said.

"In New York," Healy said.

"Or we could dig her up," Jesse said.

"Carey," Healy said. "Nice idea. I talked to the ME already. Without knowing when they died and how long they were refrigerated . . ."

Healy shook his head.

"Not worth the trouble," Jesse said.

"No."

Healy tipped his chair back slightly on its hind legs and teetered there, keeping his balance with one foot on Jesse's desk, rocking slightly.

"Well," Jesse said. "Whoever did it knew about the dream house on Stiles Island."

"Did they follow them there and kill them?" Healy said. "And see the walk-in refrigerator and improvise?"

"Or did they know about it ahead of time, and kill them there in order to refrigerate them?"

"No blood anywhere else in the house," Healy said.

"None we could find," Jesse said. "We looked hard."

"So either shot in the walk-in cooler," Healy said, "or shot someplace else and dumped there."

"Which would account for the small amount of blood," Jesse said.

"They could have been shot there, and the killer cleaned up."

"And missed the minuscule amounts we picked up with the blue light," Jesse said.

"They'd have bled a lot when they were shot," Healy said.

"And bled for a while," Jesse said. "You'd have had to do several clean-ups."

"Having, under this theory, just murdered two people," Healy said, "with no certain assurance that nobody heard the shots."

They were both quiet for a time.

"I like it better that they were shot somewhere else and moved there after they died," Jesse said.

"And the blood traces were just a little postmortem seepage."

"Yes."

Again the two men were quiet.

Then Healy said, "Yeah. Me too. Which means that whoever did them knew about the house."

"Which they bought under her maiden name to keep it a secret."

"Which makes Lutz look pretty good for it," Healy said.

"It does," Jesse said. "On the other hand, a lot of money changed hands."

"So maybe his lawyer knew," Healy said.

"Or his manager," Jesse said.

"Or one of the wives."

"Swell," Jesse said. "We've got all the suspects we had before."

"We?" Healy said. "Whaddya mean, 'we'? I'm just stopping by on my way from work."

Jesse nodded.

"Thank you for your support," he said.

They were drinking white wine by the window, at the table in Sunny's kitchen, in the little bay, when Spike came into the loft with the stalker. From under the table Rosie gave her ferocious gurgling bark. Jenn took in a sudden breath and froze. The stalker was a middle-sized well-dressed man in his middle thirties with a neat beard. He face was rigid, and very pale.

"Timothy Patrick Lloyd," Spike said, "according to his driver's license. Lives in the Prudential Center. His business cards say he's the CEO of Spot-on Marketing. He's got six twenties in his wallet."

"You've met Spike," Sunny said. "I'm Sunny Randall, and, I assume, you know this young woman."

Lloyd's eyes were busy. He looked at Sunny, shifted to Jenn, looked quickly away, scanned the loft. Rosie came out from under the table and sniffed at his pant leg. He looked down at her and away. Jenn continued to stare at him.

"He doesn't have a weapon," Spike said, and closed the door and leaned on it.

Sunny said, "So tell us your story, Mr. Lloyd."

"I'm here against my will," Lloyd said.

His voice was thin and tight. Sunny nodded at the phone on the kitchen counter.

"Feel free to call the police," Sunny said. "Nine-one-one would work."

Lloyd's eyes shifted to the phone and back.

"I just want to leave," he said.

"You do know Ms. Stone," Sunny said.

He didn't look at Jenn.

"She's on Channel Three," he said.

"And Jenn, you know Mr. Lloyd," Sunny said.

"No," Jenn said.

"But you recognize him."

"No."

"He's been following you around," Sunny said, "since I met you."

"I don't think it's him," Jenn said.

"It is," Sunny said.

Sunny looked at Spike.

"It is," Spike said.

"I've never followed anyone," Lloyd said.

"I don't know him," Jenn said.

"Did he rape you?" Sunny said.

"Rape?" Lloyd said. "Rape. Jesus Christ, I never raped anybody."

"No," Jenn said. "He didn't."

"He didn't rape you."

"No."

"What the hell is this?" Lloyd said.

"I could probably convince him to tell us his side of things," Spike said.

"What are you going to do?" Lloyd said.

"Vee have our vays," Spike said.

Sunny saw Lloyd's fists clenched at his sides. A touching moment of bravado, Sunny thought. Sunny had seen Spike in action. Lloyd had no chance. Sunny shook her head.

"He didn't rape you," Sunny said to Jenn.

"No," Jenn said.

She had looked at no one since Spike brought Lloyd in.

"Did anyone rape you?" Sunny said.

"Of course someone raped me," Jenn said.

"And someone is stalking you," Sunny said.

"Yes. Don't you believe me?"

Sunny looked at Spike. He shrugged and stepped away from the door.

"You're free to go, Mr. Lloyd," Sunny said.

Lloyd started to speak, looked at Spike, and said nothing. Spike opened the door, and Lloyd went out. Sunny looked down at Rosie, who was sitting by the kitchen counter, looking hopefully upward. Spike closed the door after Lloyd. He went to the counter and opened a cookie jar and gave a dog biscuit to Rosie.

"Well, don't you?" Jenn said. "Don't you believe me?"

Rosie chewed up her dog biscuit. Sunny reached down to pat her. Then she looked up at Jenn.

"The question's too hard for me, at the moment," Sunny said.

J esse talked with Conrad Lutz in the coffee shop of the
Langham Hotel.

"You're still around."

"Yeah," Lutz said. "The family wanted me to sort of stay
around until there was some sort of closure on the case."

"They paying the tab?" Jesse said.

"They are," Lutz said.

"At the Langham."

"Well, I'm already here," Lutz said. "You know?"

"Nice duty," Jesse said.

"Sure."

Lutz stirred some sugar into his coffee.

"You didn't mention a prior connection to Weeks," Jesse said.

"How prior?" Lutz said.

"You busted him for public indecency in White Marsh, Maryland, in 1987."

Lutz nodded slowly.

"Not bad," he said.

"Why didn't you mention it?" Jesse said.

"I was supposed to be his bodyguard. I wasn't supposed to be going around telling tales on the poor bastard."

Jesse nodded.

"Tell me about it," he said.

"I was with the Baltimore County police, patrolling the White Marsh Mall. A couple of women came up to me and complained of what was happening in a car in the parking lot. I checked it out and it was Weeks and some kid doing the nasty in his car. I'd have chased them off and let it slide, but the two ladies raised hell and insisted I arrest them for defiling the mall parking lot or something. So I took them in."

"How'd he handle it?" Jesse said.

"He was embarrassed," Lutz said. "But I think he knew he could fix it. He pointed out that the girl was of age, and then he started asking me about being a cop and did I see much of this and that sort of thing."

Jesse nodded. A waitress came by and freshened their coffee.

"Some of it was schmoozing," Lutz said. "You know, be pals with you, how you see they're not afraid, and no hard feelings. But in fact he actually seemed interested. Few weeks later he called and asked if we could talk."

"What did he want to talk about?"

"Police work," Lutz said. "Weeks was going to do a full-hour commentary on his TV show about police work, and wanted to research it. I said okay. By that time the lewd-behavior charge had sort of gone away. So I talked with him. He rode around in the cruiser with me. I liked him. He was a pretty nice guy. You know? He was interested in everything. He wasn't full of himself. He seemed to get it. He never got in the way. And finally, when he did the commentary, I liked that, too. He was fair. He didn't whitewash cops. But he didn't blackball us, either. He knew the score."

"He mention being arrested for public lewdness?"

Lutz grinned and shook his head.

"He was honest," Lutz said. "But he wasn't crazy."

"How'd you end up as his bodyguard?" Jesse said.

"He got some death threats. Never clear who they were from. Weeks said that telling the truth in public was inherently risky."

"So he called you?"

"Yeah. We'd become pretty friendly. We used to talk now and then. Have dinner once in a while. He offered a lot more than Baltimore County was paying. So I went with him."

"Any follow-up on the death threats?"

"Not till now," Lutz said.

"You think this murder is about that?"

"I don't know what this murder is about," Lutz said.

Jesse nodded.

"I talked with the doormen here," Jesse said.

"Yeah?"

"No one remembers seeing Walton and Carey walking up Franklin Street," Jesse said.

"Why would they?" Lutz said.

"Nobody remembers you asking about it, either."

"For crissake, Jesse, they talk to a hundred people a day."

"Do you remember specifically who you talked with?" Jesse said.

Lutz shook his head.

"Not really. White guy," he said. "Looked Irish. You know, they all look the same in the monkey suit."

"Not many Irish doormen around the city," Jesse said. "If we got them all together, could you pick him out?"

"Probably not, it was a while ago. I just don't remember."

"But someone did see them that day," Jesse said.

"That's what he told me."

"And you can't remember which one it was you talked with."

Lutz shook his head.

"I should, I know, me being a former cop and all. But . . ." He spread his hands. "You know how it is."

"Actually, I don't," Jesse said.

Lutz shrugged. Jesse waited. Lutz didn't say anything else.

After a time, Jesse broke the silence.

"You know anything about any real estate that Weeks might have been interested in around here?" he said.

"Real estate?" Lutz said. "Walton? No, I don't know anything about that."

Jesse nodded.

"Why do you ask?" Lutz said.

Jesse shook his head.

"You got something breaking in the case?" Lutz said.

"My ass, mostly," Jesse said.

T he window in Jesse's hotel room looked out onto an air shaft on the West Side of New York. Jesse made a drink and looked at the air shaft for a time. Then he went to the phone and called Sunny Randall.

"How's your hotel?" she said.

"A bed, running water," Jesse said.

"You've always been a minimalist."

"I'm on a minimalist budget," Jesse said.

"How's the case?"

"Lot of information, none of it useful," Jesse said. "How about yours?"

"Weird," Sunny said.

"Good to hear," Jesse said.

He sipped his drink.

"I'm sorry," Sunny said.

"I didn't expect it wouldn't be," Jesse said. "How weird is it?"

"You know my friend Spike."

"Yes."

"We decided that it was time to put Jenn and the stalker together," Sunny said. "In a protected environment."

"And?"

"Spike, ah, apprehended him, and brought him to my place."

"And?"

"They swore they didn't know each other," Sunny said. "He didn't know her. He wasn't stalking her. He was an innocent bystander."

"Jenn?"

"She said the same thing. He wasn't the stalker. He didn't rape her. She'd never seen him before in her life."

Jesse took another drink. He did it carefully so that maybe Sunny wouldn't hear the ice clink.

"Any chance that it's the truth?" Jesse said.

"I don't know about the rape," Sunny said. "But this guy has been stalking her. I spotted him. Spike spotted him. He'd been grabbed by this very large man and brought to a strange place against his will. I offered him a chance to call the police. He didn't. Plus, he runs a marketing company that does business with Jenn's TV station. He's bought a lot of time there."

"On-air people wouldn't have to know the advertisers."

"No."

"But why would she deny the stalking?" Jesse said.

"I was going to ask you."

Jesse looked at his glass. Still plenty left. He glanced at the dark air shaft outside. At her end of the phone, Sunny was quiet.

"When I was about as bad as I've ever been with drinking," Jesse said, "I snuck it. I didn't drink in front of Jenn. She thought I was quitting. But I used to keep a pint of scotch in my car, and have a few pops when I was alone. One day we were going someplace and Jenn opened the glove compartment and there was this half-empty bottle of booze. . . ."

Jesse sipped some scotch.

"And she said, 'Why is this bottle of scotch in the glove compartment?' . . . and I looked at it and said, 'What bottle of scotch?'"

"You were caught in something you were ashamed of and you didn't know what to do," Sunny said.

"It happens," Jesse said. "You get caught and you're humiliated. It's too horrible, and you say anything. You deny the fact before you."

"You think she made this up?" Sunny said.

"I don't know."

"Why would she make it up?" Sunny said.

"I don't know."

Jesse's room was dark. The small light that had come from the air shaft had disappeared with the day. He put his head back against the cheap fabric covering of his chair.

"I'm going to find out," Sunny said.

Jesse didn't speak.

"Focus on the murders," Sunny said. "I'll do this."

Jesse finished his glass. He looked at the bottle. Plenty left.

"There's a key to her apartment in the drawer of my desk in the police station. It's labeled."

"Will you clear me with Molly?" Sunny said.

"Yes."

"I'll go get the key," she said.

They were both quiet.

"We had a good time in Los Angeles," Jesse said after a time.

"Yes. Things change," Sunny said.

"Sometimes."

They were quiet again.

"I think it's time for us to hang up," Sunny said.

"Yes."

"I'll talk to you tomorrow."

"Good," Jesse said.

They hung up. Jesse sat motionless for a time, holding the empty glass.

"We'll always have Beverly Hills," he said out loud in the silent room.

After a time, Jesse turned on the light next to the bed. Then he stood and made himself another drink. He took it to the window and looked at the air shaft. Then he turned and walked to the dresser and looked at himself in the mirror. The reflection was shadowed by the single light.

"A second-rate hotel with a window on an air shaft," he said, staring into the mirror. "And a bottle of scotch."

He raised his glass to his reflection.

"Perfect," he said, and drank some scotch.

J esse had lunch with Stephanie Weeks in the hotel coffee shop. The room was noisy with families. Scattered among them were a few businessmen, sitting alone, hunched over their meals. Stephanie ordered a Grey Goose martini. Jesse had coffee.

"You don't drink?" she said.

"Not at lunch," Jesse said.

"You're actually staying here?" Stephanie said.

"Yep."

"I don't think I've ever known anyone who stayed here."

"The poor sometimes have to travel," Jesse said.

"Oh, yes. I'm sorry. I must have sounded so snooty."

"A little snooty," Jesse said. "We have a bit of new information about the murders and we're reinterviewing everyone."

"What is your new information?" Stephanie said.

"We were wrong on the time of death. When is the last time you saw Mr. Weeks?"

"Oh God, I don't know. A year? I mean, we were divorced a long time ago. We aren't enemies, but we're not pals. . . ." Stephanie smiled faintly.

The waitress came with salads. Stephanie ordered a second martini.

"Goes good with salad," Jesse said.

"Goes good with anything," Stephanie said.

"Why the smile?" Jesse said. "When you said you weren't pals?"

"Except once in a while," Stephanie said. "We're pals."

"How so?"

Stephanie smiled again.

"Old times' sake?" she said.

"What did you do?" Jesse said. "For old times' sake."

"Well," Stephanie said. "Aren't you nosy."

"I'm the police," Jesse said. "I'm supposed to be nosy."

Stephanie colored a little. The waitress returned with her martini. She sipped it and took out an olive and ate that.

"Sometimes I think it's all about the olives," Stephanie said.

"So what did you do, for old times' sake?" Jesse said.

"Walton was in many ways a sexual athlete," Stephanie said. "He never tired. He never ejaculated. He could do sex, it seems, forever."

"Not always a bad thing," Jesse said.

"Twice a year, it was good," Stephanie said. "Not on a daily basis."

"Did his failure to ejaculate bother him?" Jesse said.

"He never said."

"Even when you were married?"

"Children were an issue early on, but then . . ." She spread her hands and shook her head.

"His current wife know about this?"

"About me?" Stephanie said. "I don't know. I was the least of her problems anyway."

"He was a philanderer," Jesse said.

"Relentless," Stephanie said. "But, hell, so was she."

"Lorrie?" Jesse said.

"Sure."

"Revenge?" Jesse said.

"Maybe, but I think she would have fooled around even if Walton were Goody Two-shoes."

"She promiscuous or did she have a favorite?" Jesse said.

"I don't know. I didn't follow it all that closely. Tom Nolan said she was pretty hot and heavy with Alan Hendricks."

"The researcher."

"You could call him that," Stephanie said.

"What else could you call him?"

"Power behind the throne."

"Tell me about that," Jesse said.

"More and more, Alan did not only the research but the writing. More and more he decided what the subject matter would be. More and more he was doing the interviews, and writing the stuff, and Walton would say it."

"How do you know," Jesse said.

"Tom Nolan."

"You're friendly with him."

Stephanie smiled again.

"Yes, I am," she said.

"How's Tom's staying power?"

Stephanie smiled widely.

"Sufficient," she said.

Jesse smiled with her.

"How come you didn't tell me all this stuff when we talked before?" he said.

"In front of all those people?"

He nodded.

"What else is there?" I said.

Stephanie drank the rest of her martini. She hadn't yet eaten any of her salad.

"He left me ten thousand dollars in his will," she said.

"Old times' sake," Jesse said.

"He left ten thousand dollars to Ellen, too."

"And the rest?" Jesse said.

Stephanie was looking for the waitress. When she saw her she gestured with her empty glass.

"Lorrie," she said.

"How much?"

"Thirty million, give or take. Plus the whole Walton Weeks enterprise."

"Is that worth anything without Walton?"

"There's always Alan."

"TV, radio, the whole thing?" Jesse said.

Stephanie ate a bite of her salad. The martini came. She turned her attention back to it.

"I don't know. You'd need to ask Tom about that."

"Nolan, the manager," Jesse said.

"Yes, and Sam."

"Gates? The lawyer?"

"Uh-huh."

"Nothing in the will about Carey Longley," Jesse said.

"No."

If the martinis were affecting Stephanie, she showed no sign of it. Except that she had slowed down on the third one, interspersing a sip with the ingestion of salad. The hotel coffee shop was not a place of lingering luncheons, and most of the tables had emptied.

"Do you know Conrad Lutz?" Jesse said.

"I've heard the name. He was Walton's bodyguard, wasn't he?"

"He wasn't with Walton when you were?" Jesse said.

"No."

"Do you know any reason," Jesse said, "why Walton would need a bodyguard?"

"Well, he annoyed some important people, certainly. But, no, not really. When I was with him he never seemed to need one."

"Who would," Jesse said.

thought I'd ask Sam to sit in with us," Tom Nolan said.
"If you think you need a lawyer," Jesse said.

"I'm an entertainment lawyer," Sam Gates said. "If we were concerned about criminal matters, I wouldn't be the one."

"It's just that I know Walton's business from one side," Nolan said. "And Sam from the other."

"Sure," Jesse said. "What's the future for Walton's business now?"

"We plan to carry forward with Alan," Nolan said.

"Hendricks?" Jesse said.

"Yes. The enterprise will still be called Walton Weeks, but now it will be Walton Weeks, with Alan Hendricks."

"The market will bear that?" Jesse said.

"Yes. Alan has sat in for Walton in the past. People like him. We'll market it as the legacy renewed."

"So the beat goes on," Jesse said.

"Of course there's only one Walton Weeks," Nolan said. "But yes, the enterprise will continue."

"And this was predictable?"

Nolan looked at Gates.

"Predictable?" Gates said.

"If I told you last winter that Weeks would die, would you have known that the, ah, enterprise would survive?"

"Well, of course, no one was thinking about that last winter," Gates said. "Walton was not an old man. He was in good health."

"But if you had thought about it?" Jesse said.

"I assume we would have concluded that the franchise was still viable," Gates said.

"That would, of course, have been up to Mrs. Weeks," Jesse said.

"Of course," Gates answered. "She being the sole heir."

"And she's in Hendricks's corner," I said.

"She thinks Alan would be a suitable replacement," Gates said.

"Would it have been apparent that she thought so six months ago?" Jesse said.

"What are you getting at?" Nolan said.

Jesse smiled and shrugged.

"I'm just floundering," Jesse said. "You know, small-town cop in over my head."

"I'm sure you're doing your best," Gates said.

Jesse looked grateful.

"So did Lorrie and Alan get along okay?"

"Yes," Nolan said. "Of course."

"How well?" Jesse said.

Nolan looked away.

Gates said, "Are you implying something?"

"To imply something," Jesse said, "you have to know something. I'm just trying to learn."

"I doubt that either Tom or I could speak to their private lives," Gates said.

"And the question of how well did they get along," Jesse said, "is about their private lives?"

"I didn't say that," Gates said.

"How about Lorrie and Walton?" Jesse said.

Nolan looked at Gates again. Gates was silent.

Then he said, "You're a pretty good small-town cop."

Jesse smiled.

"Well," he said. "I am the chief."

Gates nodded.

"How were Mr. and Mrs. Weeks getting on?" Jesse said.

"May we be off the record here?"

"No," Jesse said. "I won't talk about anything to the press. But if I have evidence, I will share it with the DA."

"But no press."

"Not from me," Jesse said.

Gates nodded again. Jesse waited.

"Walton asked me to refer him to a divorce lawyer," Gates said.

"He did?" Nolan said.

No one paid him any attention.

"When?" Jesse said.

"Three months ago."

"And did you?"

"Yes," Gates said.

"Who?"

"I believe that would be covered by privilege," Gates said.

"No doubt," Jesse said. "Of course, the client is murdered and I'm trying to find who did it."

Gates nodded. "That would be a consideration," he said.

Jesse waited.

"Esther Bergman," Gates said.

"She here in the city?"

"Yes. Hoffman, Dalton, and Berks," Gates said. "Downtown."

"Did he consult her?" Jesse said.

"I don't know."

"Was Mrs. Weeks aware?"

"I don't know."

The three men were quiet for a time in Nolan's penthouse office.

"What effect would a divorce have had on the enterprise?" Jesse said finally.

Nolan looked at Gates. Gates nodded.

"None, would be my guess," Nolan said. "Walton was a name brand. He'd been divorced before. I don't think it would have had any effect."

"And on the former Mrs. Weeks?" Jesse said.

"Lorrie?" Nolan said. "I suppose that would have depended on the settlement."

"But she would be unlikely to remain an heir."

"Unlikely," Gates said.

Jenn's apartment was clean, but it wasn't neat. Clothes were scattered about. The dirty dishes and scattered crumbs of a small and hurried breakfast were in the kitchen. There was a chaos of makeup in the bathroom and a wet towel wadded on the floor near the shower. Sunny smiled.

*Running late this morning.*

In the bedroom, on the bureau, was a big picture of Jesse. He was hatless and the sun was full on his face. Sunny looked at the picture for a time. Then she went back to the living room and sat at the little painted writing table with French legs that Jenn appeared to use as a desk. There was a phone on the desk and a laptop computer, open, the screen lit. Sunny opened the address book at the bottom of the screen. There were a lot of addresses. Jesse's e-mail address was there. And so was tpat@cybercop.com, which when she clicked on it proved to be Timothy Patrick Lloyd.

*That was easy.*

The smell of Jenn's perfume was strong in the apartment. The place was expensive and, Sunny thought, a little overdecorated.

*Well, I'm here. I might as well learn what I can.*

She opened the drawer in the writing table. It was like most people's desk drawers. Pens, paper clips, papers that weren't necessary but couldn't be thrown away yet, a ruler, a box of notepaper, some scissors, a roll of stamps. In the small second drawer was a checkbook and some bills. Systematically, Sunny went through the apartment. In a drawer in the buffet in the dining area, she found a photo album/scrapbook. There were pictures of Jenn and Jesse at their wedding. There were several different pictures of Jenn with several different men, one of whom was a recognizable actor. There was a picture of Jesse, very young, in a baseball uniform. And a clipping from the newspaper about Jesse's part in the capturing of two serial killers in Paradise several years ago. There were pictures of Jenn on air, and publicity head shots of her. There were also two pictures of Jenn, in a bikini, with Timothy Patrick Lloyd, on a beach somewhere.

Sunny took the two pictures and put them in her purse. She went through the rest of the album. There were no family pictures in the album. No one who appeared to be a parent. No pictures of Jenn as a child. Sunny put the album back. In Jenn's bedroom closet was nightwear from Victoria's Secret. The lingerie in her dresser drawer had been selected for appearance far more than comfort. Sunny smiled to herself.

The medicine cabinet had a partly used package of birth-control patches. The makeup was expensive and showed thought. The perfume was very good. The hair products were mostly what Sunny used. The hot-roller device was the same one Sunny had.

*She's not that different. Looks good. Wants to look better. Nothing remarkable, except she's a liar.*

Sunny stood for a few moments in the silent living room and looked around. The apartment was new and stylish, and clean and careless and ordinary and still. Sunny spoke aloud, her voice much too real in the empty space.

"God, I'm glad I have Rosie," her voice said.

44

Walton Weeks Enterprises had offices in a building near Penn Station. There were several secretaries in a big front space, Walton's imposing office, now bearing silent witness in the corner, and a somewhat smaller but still substantial office beside it where Jesse sat with Alan Hendricks.

"You nervous?" Jesse said.

"Excuse me?"

"You're about to become Walton Weeks," Jesse said. "Does that make you nervous."

"Well," Hendricks said. "They are certainly big shoes to fill."

"Of course, you've walked some distance in them already," Jesse said.

Hendricks's face looked stiff to Jesse.

"Meaning?" Hendricks said.

"Well, you have done a lot of Walton's research and writing," Jesse said. "Have you not?"

"Well, of course, I've been with him for some years."

"And you're prepared to proceed, alone," Jesse said.

"If Mrs. Weeks wants me to."

"Does she?"

"She has suggested as much," Hendricks said.

He looked humble.

"And you get along," Jesse said.

"She's a very fine woman," Alan said. "I hope I don't disappoint her."

"Have you ever?"

"I don't think so."

Jesse smiled and didn't say anything.

"What are you implying," Hendricks said.

Jesse shrugged.

"Maybe you're inferring?"

Hendricks stared at Jesse.

"I have interviewed half a dozen heads of state," Hendricks said. "If you think I'm going to be intimidated by some small-town police chief, you are sadly mistaken."

"Damn," Jesse said.

"Why are we having this conversation?"

"The time-of-death issue has opened up," Jesse said. "I suppose you have an alibi for the last six weeks?"

"Six weeks," Hendricks said. "That's a joke. I thought you had time of death established."

"We thought so, too," Jesse said. "But we didn't."

"So you now come here on some sort of fishing expedition, implying something illicit between me and Lorrie Weeks?"

"I don't recall suggesting that," Jesse said.

"I know what you're doing," Hendricks said. "I'm not some scared teenager you've stopped for speeding."

"I guess not," Jesse said. "So were you intimate with Mrs. Weeks?"

Hendricks stood suddenly up behind his desk.

"This interview is over," Hendricks said.

Jesse stood more slowly. He smiled and nodded.

"You were," he said. "Weren't you."

Hendricks said nothing. Jesse turned and left. *Stephanie had that one right,* Jesse thought as he waited for the elevator.

**45**

S uit brought a box of donuts and three coffees with him into the squad room. He put the box in the middle of the conference table and gave a cup each to Molly Crane and Jesse.

"I miss anything?" Suit said.

"I was outlining my theory of the crime," Jesse said.

"Which is?" Suit said.

"That we're not solving it," Molly said.

Suit nodded.

"Cox is on the front desk," Suit said. "He wanted to know how come he didn't get donuts. I told him because he hadn't made detective yet."

"Good, Suit," Molly said. "Promote unit cohesion."

Jesse took the plastic cover off his coffee and tossed it onto the conference table. He stood beside the green chalkboard where he had written a list of names in yellow chalk.

"I talked to the divorce lawyer," Jesse said. "Esther Bergman. She affirms that Weeks wanted a divorce. That he was prepared to make a generous settlement on Lorrie, but that he didn't want alimony and he would, of course, change his will."

"Any of this happen?" Molly said.

"No, the lawyer was in process."

"Lorrie Weeks know?" Suit said.

"The lawyer said she did."

"Funny no one mentioned this," Suit said.

"Good old Stephanie," Jesse said.

"What else did you find out this trip?" Suit said.

"Lorrie was having sex with Hendricks," Jesse said, "the faithful researcher."

"How'd you find that out?" Suit said.

"Good old Stephanie," Molly said. "Jesse employed the three-martini-lunch interrogation."

"Often effective," Jesse said.

"Unless the interrogator joins in," Molly said.

"Stephanie allowed me to know as well that she was occasionally intimate with Walton, and currently with Tom Nolan."

"Busy group down there in New York," Molly said.

"Lot of people been not telling us a lot of stuff," Suit said. "Like Lutz didn't mention that he had busted Weeks in Baltimore County."

"A hazard of police work," Jesse said.

"Makes you get sort of distrustful," Suit said.

Molly broke a small piece off a glazed cruller.

"You think?" she said, and put the piece of cruller in her mouth.

"So what we do have is that Mrs. Weeks knows her husband is planning to divorce her. She is intimate with the man who will continue the franchise after her husband's death."

"You're sure Stephanie's not just being catty?" Molly said.

"Isn't catty a sexist concept?" Jesse said.

"It is," Molly said. "You're sure she's not?"

"I talked with Hendricks. They were doing something," Jesse said.

"But if he divorces her," Suit says, "then she loses control of the franchise."

"Which might mean she loses Hendricks," Molly said. "Or Hendricks doesn't get the job when Weeks dies."

Jesse nodded.

"Or both," he said.

"Carey and the unborn child get it all?" Molly said.

"I would assume," Jesse said.

"So there's some pretty good motive here," Suit said.

Jesse nodded. No one said anything for a moment. Then Molly said, "But?"

"But can you see them doing it?"

"I don't even know them," Molly said.

She ate another small piece of cruller. Jesse smiled. Jenn used to eat something in small pieces so it wouldn't be fattening.

"Bergdorf's sophisticate, adult Ivy Leaguer," Jesse said. "Princeton probably. They could shoot a couple of people maybe. But transport them to a house with a walk-in refrigerator and store them there, then haul them out and hang one up and toss the other in a Dumpster?"

"Don't seem like people who would be that aware of the effects of ambient temperature on a corpse," Molly said.

"That's right," Jesse said.

"But Lutz would," Suit said.

"That's right," Jesse said.

"But he's got no motive," Suit said.

"He has no motive that we know about," Jesse said.

"They could have hired him to do it," Molly said.

"And he'd own them for the rest of their lives," Jesse said.

"Even Bergdorf sophisticates and Princeton grads can be stupid," Molly said.

Jesse nodded.

"So," Suit said. "Now we have an actual theory of the crime."

"Lorrie, with or without the complicity of Hendricks, did it, maybe with help from Lutz."

"Lot of with or withouts and maybes in there," Molly said.

"How true," Jesse said.

"And do we have any hard evidence to support our theory?" Molly said.

"You mean like clues?" Jesse said.

Molly nodded.

"No," Jesse said.

"So what do we do now."

"We go back into everybody's history," Jesse said.

"Everybody?" Suit said.

"Everybody on the chalkboard," Jesse said.

"And of course we may find out that Lutz is telling the truth."

"However ineptly," Jesse said.

"And that Lorrie and Alan are simply adulterers. People cheat on their spouses without killing them, you know."

Jesse smiled at her. "From experience, Moll?"

"Not yet."

"Well, when you're ready . . ." Jesse said.

"You're on the list, Jesse."

"How about me," Suit said. "Am I on the list."

"Not till you're old enough," Molly said.

"For crissake, Moll, I'm almost a detective."

"So we have a theory, let's see if we can find something that proves it or disproves it," Jesse said.

"Wow," Molly said. "Like the scientific method."

"Sort of," Jesse said.

"What's the scientific method?" Suit said.

"And you wonder why you're not on the list," Molly said. She finished her cruller.

"I don't know why I bother to eat these," she said. "I might as well apply them directly to my hips."

Sunny sat at the bar with Jesse in the Gray Gull. She put the pictures of Jenn and Timothy Patrick Lloyd on the bar.

"You recognize Jenn," Sunny said. "The guy she's with is the stalker."

Jesse drank some scotch.

"Who she denies knowing," he said.

"And who denies knowing her," Sunny said.

Sunny looked at Jesse's face as he stared down at the pictures. His face showed nothing. The couple in the pictures was embracing.

"They are not strangers," Jesse said.

"No."

"You have a plan?" Jesse said.

"My plan was to see what you thought I should do."

Jesse nodded. She wondered how it must feel for him, looking at the pictures of Jenn with another man. It wasn't like a surprise, but it had to be painful, Sunny thought. She sipped her martini and looked at him over the rim. He was still looking at the pictures. His face was empty.

"I guess we need to confront her with these pictures," Jesse said.

"I can do that," Sunny said.

"No," Jesse said. "I need to do it."

"Why?"

"It'll be easier for her," he said.

"For you to catch her in deceit instead of me?"

Jesse nodded.

"She'll be less mortified," he said.

Sunny didn't say anything.

"Imagine if it were Richie," Jesse said. "Wouldn't you want to do it?"

"Proving that I'm crazy," Sunny said, "doesn't prove that you're not."

"I know."

"She . . ." Sunny started and stopped.

"I know," Jesse said.

They both drank.

"Is there anything she could do that would make you give her up?" Sunny said.

"I don't know," Jesse said. "For a while there, when we were in L.A. together . . ."

"I remember," Sunny said. "And now?"

Jesse stared into his drink.

"I love you, Sunny," he said. "Hell, I probably love Molly Crane."

"Whom you've never touched," Sunny said.

"Of course not."

"But Jenn is Jenn," Sunny said.

"Yes."

"God save me," Sunny said. "I understand this."

"I know you do," Jesse said.

He finished his drink and motioned for a refill.

"So what do you want me to do with her?" Sunny said.

"Stay with her," Jesse said.

Sunny nodded. She finished her drink and nodded to the bartender.

"When will you have time to talk with her?" Sunny said.

Jesse smiled slightly and shook his head.

"I can make time," he said. "It's when will I have the strength."

From his window, looking down over the driveway of the fire station, Jesse watched the arrival. The governor of the Commonwealth, his man Richard Kennfield, and three suits whose function Jesse did not know got out of a trooper-driven limo and moved through the press of reporters toward Jesse's office. A big black Chevy Suburban parked behind the limo. No one got out.

The governor stopped to talk with a gaggle of television reporters. Jesse couldn't hear what he said. Probably something forceful and positive. Then he and his cluster moved into the station and came to Jesse's office. The governor stuck out his hand.

"Chief Stone?" he said. "I'm Cabot Forbes."

Jesse shook his hand. The governor looked around.

Kennfield said, "The governor would like his staff with him. Is there a bigger room?"

"Sure," Jesse said.

They went down to the conference room. Jesse moved an empty pizza box off the table and gestured for the group to sit down. He sat at one end of the table. The governor stood at the other. He was tall with close-cut gray hair and a thin face.

"We're here to help," the governor said. "Not to criticize."

Jesse nodded.

"But this case has dragged on long enough to become an embarrassment to the Commonwealth, and the people of the Commonwealth need to know that there's an end in sight."

Jesse nodded. The governor paused, and when Jesse didn't say anything, he looked a little annoyed.

"This is made more embarrassing because I count both Walton and Lorrie as personal friends," the governor said.

Jesse nodded.

"Is there progress?" the governor said.

"Yes."

"Do you have a suspect?"

"Many," Jesse said.

"Is an arrest imminent?"

"No."

"What do you need to bring this case to a close?"

"Clues," Jesse said.

"Are you being deliberately uncooperative, Chief Stone?"

"No, sir. I'm listening attentively."

"I am especially concerned that Mrs. Weeks be treated with every consideration," the governor said. "This has been a nightmare for her and she deserves closure."

Jesse nodded.

"For God's sake, Stone, I was at their wedding."

"Really," Jesse said. "When did they get married?"

The governor looked at Kennfield.

"Nineteen ninety," Kennfield said.

"Where?"

"Baltimore, wasn't it," the governor said to Kennfield.

Kennfield nodded.

"At the Harbor Court," he said.

"How'd they meet?" Jesse said.

Again, the governor looked at Kennfield.

"Oddly enough, through Walton's bodyguard," Kennfield said. "He introduced them."

"Lutz?" Jesse said.

"Yes," Kennfield said, "Conrad Lutz."

"How did he know Lorrie," Jesse said.

Both the governor and Kennfield shook their heads.

"Let me remind you," the governor said, "that I am the chief executive of this state. I'm not going to be sidetracked.

I came here in good faith to offer the complete resources of the Commonwealth to expedite this investigation."

"Thank you, sir," Jesse said.

"Stone," Forbes said, "can you cut out the 'Yes sir no sir thank you sir' crap for one minute. Are you getting anywhere on this goddamned case or not."

"I'm doing what I can, Governor," Jesse said. "And I'm pretty good at it. As soon as there's an arrest, I'll be in touch."

The governor reddened slightly and looked at Kennfield again.

Then he said, "We'll hold you to that," and wheeled and walked out of the room. The staff hustled to pick up their notebooks and briefcases and followed him out.

L utz checked out," Suit said when he came into Jesse's office.

"When?"

"Day after you last talked with him," Suit said. "I tried his New York address. He doesn't answer the phone. I talked to the building manager, and he talked to the doorman, and they haven't seen Lutz."

"Well, something started moving," Jesse said.

"Except we don't know where, or why," Suit said.

"Yet," Jesse said. "Any movement is good."

"I guess," Suit said. "We gonna find him?"

"Yes."

"We going down to New York again?"

"Maybe," Jesse said.

Jesse looked at the ceiling, as if there were something up there. Suit waited. Jesse didn't speak.

"You see the guv on TV this morning?" Suit said.

"No."

"He says he's taking a more active part in the investigation," Suit said. "Says he's bringing the full resources of his office to bear. Probably solve it by this evening."

"Maybe not," Jesse said. "See what you can find out about Lorrie Weeks, before she became Lorrie Weeks. What was her name? Where was she from? How did she know Lutz? Anything you can come up with. Probably be useful if you got a blowup of her driver's license photo from New York DMV."

"If I track her down," Suit said, "will it go in my personnel file?"

"You'll be a lock for detective," Jesse said.

"If we ever have detectives," Suit said.

"Absolutely," Jesse said. "You'll be one of them."

"What I like," Suit said, "is the guv comes up here to let the press look at him and blows a lot of smoke about how he wants the case solved, and the only thing he did helpful he doesn't even know it."

"He was annoyed that I asked about it," Jesse said.

"Just another empty shirt and tie," Suit said. "Why the hell are they all like that."

Jesse shrugged and shook his head.

"It's the kind of guy the job attracts."

"No good guys?"

"Few," Jesse said. "Would you want to be governor?"

"No."

"President?"

"Christ, no," Suit said.

"Why not?"

"Too much bullshit," Suit said.

"So who would want that kind of a job?" Jesse said.

"A bullshitter," Suit said.

Jesse smiled at him.

"If you're good with a hammer," Jesse said, "you look for a nail."

"Wow," Suit said. "No wonder you made chief."

Jenn had dressed her apartment for Jesse's arrival. The bed was made with a dressy spread and ornamental pillows. She had lighted candles, put out crystal, filled the silver ice bucket.

She hugged him when he came in.

"Oh boy," she said. "I feel so safe with you. I mean, Sunny's great, and Spike, but I never feel with anyone the way I feel with you."

"That's probably true for me, too," Jesse said.

"With me?" Jenn said. "Safe?"

"Something," Jesse said.

They stood with their arms around each other for a moment, then stepped apart.

"What's in the envelope?" Jenn said.

"I'll show you in a while," Jesse said.

Jenn brought him a drink and one for herself and sat on one corner of the couch with her legs tucked under her. Jesse sat at the other end. Jenn raised her glass to him.

"Well," she said. "Here we are."

"Yes."

"No matter what happens," Jenn said, "somehow we keep blundering along, connected to each other."

"I know," Jesse said.

"What is wrong with us, Jesse?"

"Different things, maybe."

"What do you mean?"

"Maybe what's wrong with me isn't what's wrong with you."

"And yet," Jenn said, "here we are."

Jesse nodded. He picked up the brown envelope from the coffee table and took out two eight-by-ten photographs. Enlargements of the pictures Sunny had found. He put them down on the table side by side in front of Jenn. Jenn leaned a little forward to look at the pictures.

The moment she saw the photograph, Jenn said, "Oh!"

Jesse waited.

"What are these pictures?" Jenn said.

"You and a guy," Jesse said.

"Where'd you get them?"

Jesse shrugged.

"I don't know this man," Jenn said.

"The guy with his arm around you?" Jesse said. "This guy? With your head on his chest? Him?"

"Oh, Jesse, don't be jealous," Jenn said. "You know how I am."

"If I knew how you were for sure," Jesse said, "maybe my life would be simpler."

"I don't even know that man, we were just at some beach party somewhere. Just kidding around."

"His name is Timothy Patrick Lloyd."

"Could be," Jenn said.

"You know him?"

"Not really," Jenn said.

"His e-mail address is in your computer," Jesse said.

"My computer?"

"Tpat at cybercop-dot-com," Jesse said.

"Goddamn you, you searched my apartment."

Jesse shook his head.

"I didn't give you a key so you'd come snooping around," Jenn said.

Jesse didn't speak.

"You bastard," Jenn said.

Jesse said nothing.

"I had a nice dinner ready," she said.

She began to cry. Jesse took in some air and sat. Jenn sobbed. Jesse waited.

After a time, Jenn said to Jesse, "Give me a napkin or something."

Jesse handed her a cocktail napkin from the pretty arrange-ment on the coffee table. Jenn patted at her eyes with the napkin.

"It was going to be a nice evening," Jenn said.

Jesse nodded.

"I don't have many of those anymore," Jenn said.

Jesse nodded at the pictures on the coffee table.

"That's your stalker, Jenn."

"I don't—"

Jesse put up his hand as if stopping traffic.

"We both know it," he said. "Did he rape you?"

Jenn teared up again, and put her face in her hands and shook her head.

"No, he didn't rape you?" Jesse said.

Jenn slid down the couch and pressed against Jesse with her face against his chest. He put an arm around her. She cried quietly.

"Did he rape you?" Jesse said.

She didn't answer.

After a time, Jesse said, "There's nothing so bad I can't hear it, Jenn."

His voice was hoarse.

"We had sex, when I didn't want to," Jenn said.

Her voice was muffled against his chest.

"If that were rape," Jesse said, "most of the women in America would have a case."

Jesse could feel her head nod slightly against his chest.

"Did he rape you?" Jesse said.

"You'll never . . ."

"There's no never, Jenn. I don't know what's wrong with us. I don't know what we're doing, and I have no goddamned clue where we are going. But whatever and wherever, there's no never between us."

She raised her face a little from his chest. Her eyes were red, and her eye makeup was streaking.

"Is there an always?" she said.

Jesse looked down at her. The question hung in the silent room like blue smoke.

"Yes," Jesse said. "I don't know what kind of always, or what kind of life it implies, but yes. There will always be an always between us."

The blue smoke that was only a metaphor seemed to dissolve. Jenn put her head back against his chest. She stopped crying. They were quiet.

Then she said softly, "No. He didn't rape me."

Jesse patted her shoulder.

"I told him I'd been an actress. He was impressed," Jenn said. "He told me he'd love to use me in some of his marketing and promotion venues. Public appearances, modeling, it would have been a wonderful career boost."

Jesse continued to pat her shoulder. Jenn's voice was tranquil, as if she were talking of a happy childhood.

"So we had a little fling," she said.

Jesse nodded.

"But nothing worked out much. He didn't ever seem to have the right spot for me in what he was doing . . . and he wasn't that much fun."

They were quiet while Jenn remembered how much fun Tim Lloyd hadn't been.

"There's a lot of men like him," she said. "A surprising number of them. They're eager for sex, but not very good at it. They just want to sort of . . ." She paused, aware of Jesse.

"Wham, bam, thank you, ma'am," Jesse said.

"They're mostly interested in their own experience," Jenn said. "And they're just not very adroit."

"So sex with Tim Lloyd wasn't worth it for its own sake," Jesse said.

"God," Jenn said. "That sounds ugly."

"It is what it is," Jesse said.

"It wasn't working out," Jenn said. "The last time we were together, I told him that it wasn't."

"And?"

"He wanted to know why, so I told him."

"Including the part about not being adroit?"

"Yes."

"Ouch," Jesse said.

"He asked," Jenn said.

"And you were sick of him."

"Yes," Jenn said. "He said he wasn't going to take that answer. He said it was my fault because I never told him. He said he wanted to have sex again and I should show him what I wanted."

Jesse felt the muscles tighten in his back and shoulders. Jenn felt them, too.

"Are you all right?" she said.

"There's nothing I can't hear, Jenn. It needs to be said."

"I told him no. I told him we were talking about impulse and emotion, not, for God's sake, training."

"If he had to ask . . ." Jesse said.

"Exactly," Jenn said. "He was furious. I could tell he wanted to force me. But he was too spent. He wouldn't be able to erect, and we both knew it. Tim never had a fast recovery."

"So he left?"

"Yes, but he said he wasn't accepting what I said, and that I'd be seeing him again."

"So there was the threat of rape."

"That's what I heard," Jenn said.

"And then he began to stalk you."

"Yes."

"And you were scared and came to me claiming you had been raped."

"Yes."

"Did you think I'd kill him?"

"No, oh God no, Jesse. I was just scared, and when I'm scared I run to you."

"And you didn't identify him as the stalker because you didn't want to get caught in the lie."

She nodded her head against his chest.

"That was one reason."

"And you didn't want people to know the nature of your relationship," Jesse said.

Jenn nodded again.

"I'd been fucking him as a career move," she said.

"You were in a box," Jesse said. "You didn't want to be unprotected, and you didn't want him confronted."

"Yes."

"So what did you think was going to happen?"

"I didn't know. I was paralyzed. I just denied everything."

"I know," Jesse said.

"You remember that time in L.A. when I found the scotch in the glove compartment."

"Yes," Jesse said. "I understand."

They sat quietly. Jenn had stopped crying.

After a time, Jenn said, "What are you going to do?"

"I don't know. I'll ask Sunny to stay with you until I figure it out."

Again they were quiet.

Then Jenn said, "I've never even asked you about that murder case in Paradise."

"Coming down all over me," Jesse said.

"You didn't need me to add in my own troubles," Jenn said.

"I did," Jesse said. "I do. I just need a little time to figure everything out."

"Will you tell Sunny?"

"Yes."

Jenn nodded.

"She'll think I'm awful," Jenn said.

"Sunny doesn't make that kind of judgment," Jesse said.

"Do you love her?"

"Sort of," Jesse said.

"More than me."

Jesse took a deep breath and let it out slowly.

"Less," he said.

Jenn nodded again.

"What's going to become of us, Jesse?"

"God knows," Jesse said.

"No," Jenn said. "I don't think He does."

Suitcase Simpson came in with his notebook and sat down in front of Jesse's desk.

"Master detective," he said.

"You enjoy Baltimore?" Jesse said.

"Yeah. It's pretty cool. They got like this huge Quincy Market on the harbor. Lotta places to get crab cakes."

"You detect anything?" Jesse said.

"Besides the crab cakes?" Suit said. "Yeah. I did."

Jesse tipped his chair back and waited.

"I went to the Baltimore County police, and talked with a nice woman in the personnel department."

"You get to her right away?"

"Pretty quick. I turned on the charm."

"Wow," Jesse said.

"It helps in detective work, you know, if you're charming."

"I didn't know that," Jesse said.

"Anyway, when Lutz worked there the beneficiary of his life insurance was Lorraine Pilarcik. She was on his medical insurance, too."

"And what was her relation to him?" Jesse said.

"He listed her as his wife."

"Lorraine," Jesse said.

"It gets better," Suit said.

"Good."

"I got his address during the time he worked there and went and talked with people in his old neighborhood," Suit said. "There were three, four people that remembered both of them. They all called her Lorrie."

"Tell me you showed them the picture of Lorrie Weeks?" Jesse said.

"I did."

"And?"

"It was her."

"Suit," Jesse said, "you'll probably be chief of detectives."

"When we have a detective unit."

"Immediately after that," Jesse said.

"They hedged a little. You know what license photos are like. And they knew her like fifteen years ago. But they all thought it was her."

"Happy marriage?" Jesse said.

"As far as anyone can remember," Suit said.

"When did they get divorced?"

"Nobody knew they were divorced."

"When did they leave the old neighborhood?" Jesse said.

"Hard to pin it down, you know. But the consensus was late eighties, early nineties."

"You find any records of divorce?"

"Nope," Suit said. "Not in Baltimore. Got a marriage license issued to Walton Weeks and Lorrie Pilarcik, and a marriage announcement from *The Baltimore Sun.* August twenty-sixth, 1990."

"They could have divorced elsewhere," Jesse said.

"I thought of that," Suit said.

"Okay," Jesse said, "take your time. Enjoy it."

"I said to myself, *Why would you not get divorced locally?*"

"Because maybe they had moved to another state?" Jesse said.

"Maybe, or, I thought to myself, maybe they're looking for a quickie. And where can you get a quickie divorce?"

"Dover-Foxcroft, Maine?" Jesse said.

"Las Vegas," Suit said. "It did no harm to check."

"And?"

"Lorraine Pilarcik and Conrad Lutz got a divorce on August fifteenth, after six weeks of residency in Vegas," Suit said.

"Eleven days before she married Walton Weeks," Jesse said.

"Makes your head hurt a little," Suit said.

"It does. Did Weeks steal Lutz's wife and continue to employ him as a bodyguard?"

"Maybe Lutz is a really forgiving guy," Suit said.

"Maybe," Jesse said.

51

Jesse came into Sunny's loft at nine p.m. Rosie jumped down off Sunny's bed and hustled down the loft to see him. He picked her up and patted her stomach, and got a lap on the nose, before he put her down.

"Drink?" Sunny said.

"Sure."

They sat in her window bay with their drinks.

"Here's what's going on with Jenn," Jesse said.

As Jesse talked, Rosie came over and stared up at Sunny and yapped. Still focused on Jesse's recital, Sunny shifted a little in the chair to make room, and Rosie jumped up and wiggled around until she was comfortable.

When Jesse finished, Sunny shook her head.

"Poor thing," she said.

Jesse nodded.

"She seeing a shrink these days?" Sunny said.

"She has," Jesse said. "I don't know if she is seeing one now."

"She should," Sunny said. "I know someone."

"Not everybody can do it," Jesse said.

"She should be able to," Sunny said. "Maybe I'll talk to her about it."

Jesse shrugged.

"What would you like me to do?" Sunny said.

"I have to go to New York," Jesse said. "If you could keep her together until I get back."

"Would you like me, or Spike, to deal with Lloyd?" Sunny said.

"No," Jesse said. "I'll do that when I can. Just keep him away from her."

Sunny got Jesse another scotch, and poured herself more white wine.

"You think Lloyd is dangerous?" Sunny said.

"I doubt it. Usually stalking is all stalkers do."

"Except when they do more," Sunny said.

"Except then," Jesse said.

"We'll be there," Sunny said.

"Thank you."

"How's the double murder going?"

"It's starting to move, I think."

"That why you're going to New York?"

"Yes."

Jesse rattled the ice in his glass. Sunny sipped her wine. Rosie looked out from her spot in the chair, in back of Sunny's hip.

"What are you going to do, Jesse?" Sunny asked.

"About Jenn?"

"Yes," Sunny said. "Of course about Jenn."

"I'll take Lloyd off her back," Jesse said.

"I'm sure you will," Sunny said. "And then?"

Jesse drank some of his scotch and tilted his head back with his eyes closed while it eased down his throat.

"If I said to you," Jesse said, "'Sunny, will you marry me,' what would you say?"

"I'd say it was a lovely offer," she said.

"And would you say yes?"

Sunny was silent for a time.

Then she said, "No."

"Because?"

"Because I can't quite let go of Richie."

Jesse nodded. He drank the rest of his scotch and put the empty glass down on the little table.

"And so it goes," Jesse said.

L orrie Weeks still lived in the Village, in the condo she had shared with Walton Weeks, in a shiny new skyscraper that had gone up at the far-west end of Perry Street with a big view of the Hudson River. Jesse stood with Suit outside the building.

"We couldn't afford to live in there," Suit said, looking up at the glass towers.

"No," Jesse said.

"Fits nice into the neighborhood," Suit said.

"Like a hooker at a picnic," Jesse said.

"What are we hoping, exactly, to see?" Suit said.

"Lorrie Pilarcik Weeks," Jesse said.

"And when we see her?"

"We watch her," Jesse said.

"Because she's all we've got?"

"Exactly," Jesse said.

"And we don't know what else to do?"

"Precisely," Jesse said.

"It's great to train under a master," Suit said.

"I envy you the experience," Jesse said.

It was after five p.m. when Alan Hendricks pulled up in a cab and got out and went into Lorrie Weeks's building. At six fifteen they came out and walked up Perry Street away from the river. Jesse and Suit followed. They went into a restaurant on Greenwich Street. Jesse and Suit waited outside. At nine o'clock they came out of the restaurant, arm in arm, and walked back to the west end of Perry Street.

"Take the picture," Jesse said.

Suit took several.

They went in together. By midnight Hendricks had not come out. Jesse and Suit went to their hotel.

The next morning they were back outside Lorrie's building before nine. It was after ten when Hendricks strolled out wearing the same clothes he'd had on last night and walked up Perry Street.

"Stay with him," Jesse said to Suit. "I assume he's looking for a cab. If he is, let him go and come back here."

Jesse leaned on a yellow brick wall, in the sun, and looked at Lorrie's building. In fifteen minutes, Suit was back.

"Cab uptown," Suit said.

"Do you know uptown from downtown?" Jesse said.

"No, sir," Suit said. "But I heard him say 'uptown' to the cabbie."

Jesse nodded.

At quarter to twelve a cab stopped in front of Lorrie's building and Conrad Lutz got out.

"Aha!" Jesse said.

"Aha?" Suit said.

"It's chief talk," Jesse said. "Apprentice detectives aren't allowed to say *aha*!"

"Do you suppose he's going to spend the night, too?" Suit said.

"We'll find out," Jesse said. "Get the pictures."

Suit used the camera.

"Goddamn," Suit said. "I stand around here another day, I'm going to take root."

"I know it feels that way," Jesse said. "But generally you don't."

"I suppose it would be too big a coincidence," Suit said, "if they both came here and weren't visiting Lorrie Weeks."

"Yes," Jesse said. "It would."

Jesse and Suit stood outside, taking turns occasionally to go to a small restaurant two blocks up. Lutz stayed until late afternoon. When he came out, Suit followed him.

"Stay with him this time," Jesse said. "Find out where he lives."

"He gets a cab," Suit said, "I get a cab?"

"Yep."

"I gotta actually say 'Follow that cab' to a New York cabbie?"

"Don't worry about it," Jesse said. "He probably won't understand English anyway."

Suit went after Lutz. Jesse stayed. No one came. No one went. At six p.m. Suit came back.

"Lutz is staying at a hotel on Park Avenue South," he said.

He took his notebook out and found the page and looked at it.

"The W Union Square," Suit said. "They told me at the front desk that he was registered for the month."

"Lot of dough," Jesse said.

"Maybe Lutz has saved his pennies," Suit said.

"Maybe."

"Or maybe he knows a rich woman."

"Maybe," Jesse said.

"What's shaking here?"

"Some guy went by walking a Welsh corgi," Jesse said.

"That's exciting."

"It was downhill from there," Jesse said.

At seven in the evening Hendricks showed up carrying a bottle of wine and some French bread.

"An evening in," Suit said.

Jesse nodded.

"Lutz in the daytime and Hendricks at night?" Suit said.

"Seems so," Jesse said.

"Hot dog!" Suit said. "We gonna just keep standing here watching. I feel like one of those guys, you know, what do they call them, that likes to watch."

"Voyeur," Jesse said.

"Yeah, I'm starting to feel like a voyeur."

"They don't have to be having sex all this time," Jesse said.

"They don't?"

Jesse smiled.

"Better to think they are, I guess."

"Absolutely," Suit said. "Are we developing a plan?"

"We're awaiting developments."

"How long are we going to await?" Suit said.

"Until they occur, or we can't stand it anymore," Jesse said.

Suit shook his head sadly.

"That's pathetic," he said.

"I know," Jesse said. "But we got some nice photos."

53

Their third morning on Perry Street, Lutz didn't show up. At noon Jesse said to Suit, "See if he's still at the hotel."

Suit spoke on his cell phone for ten minutes before he broke the connection.

"Checked out this morning," Suit said. "Arranged with the concierge for a limo to the Delta Shuttle at LaGuardia."

"So he's going to Boston or Washington," Jesse said.

"That's what the concierge told me," Suit said. "He said it only flies those two places."

Jesse smiled.

"Call Molly on that thing," he said. "Tell her to see if he's registered at the Langham again. If he isn't, have her check other hotels."

Suit made the call.

When he was through he said to Jesse, "What exactly is a concierge?"

"They are to hotel guests as you are to me, Suit."

"Invaluable?"

"Something like that. Molly going to call us back?"

"Yes."

"You got call waiting on that thing?"

"Sure."

"While you're waiting for Molly, call Healy, and when you get him, gimme the phone."

"Can I tell him I'm your concierge?" Suit said.

"Just call him," Jesse said and rattled off the number. "I am going to need a New York City cop to help with the jurisdiction issue."

"And you figure Healy can help?"

"Better than wandering into the local precinct and explaining that I'm the chief of police in Paradise, Massachusetts," Jesse said.

"You don't think that would impress them?"

"It should," Jesse said. "But sometimes it doesn't."

Suit dialed Healy, and when Healy came on he said, "Hold for Chief Stone," and handed Jesse the phone.

"Hold for Chief Stone?" Healy said.

"That's Suitcase Simpson," Jesse said. "He amuses hell out of himself."

"Me too," Healy said. "Whaddya need?"

Jesse told him.

"Yeah," Healy said. "I'll make a couple calls."

Jesse handed the phone back to Suit, who broke the connection and put the phone away. The Welsh corgi went by again, walking two guys this time. Lorrie stayed in her condo.

"What do you think she's doing in there?" Suit said. "When she's not bopping Lutz or Hendricks."

"Looking at the view," Jesse said.

At three fifteen Molly called to report that Lutz had in fact returned to the Langham, where he was registered for the rest of the month.

"He was registered for the rest of the month here," Suit said.

"You check into a hotel, they usually ask when you're departing," Jesse said. "You don't know, you just give them some date down the line."

"What happens if you check out early?"

Jesse smiled again.

"They aren't allowed to hold you captive," he said.

Healy didn't know Rosa Sanchez, but he knew someone who knew her bureau commander, and her bureau commander put him in touch with the Sixth Precinct commander, who assigned her to Jesse. Rosa was a detective second grade, not very tall, quite slim, with black hair and olive skin and the lyrical hint of Hispania lurking behind her perfect English.

They met her at the Sixth Precinct station house.

"According to the precinct commander," she said as they walked out on West 10th Street, "I'm yours, as long as you need me . . . in a professional sense."

"You the newest detective?" Jesse said.

"Yes."

"So you catch all the stuff like this," Jesse said.

"I do," she said. "You ever on the job in a big city?"

"L.A.," Jesse said. "Robbery Homicide."

"Hotshot?"

"You bet," Jesse said.

"You think Bratton can make a difference out there?"

"He made a difference here," Jesse said.

"Good point," she said. "What's our plan?"

"We're going to visit a woman at her condo on Perry Street."

"Not one of the big new ones?" Rosa said.

"Yeah."

"Oh, good," she said. "I been dying to see what they're like inside."

"While we're in there, we'll conduct an interview, which Officer Simpson will covertly record."

"Is that a tape recorder that he's got in his purse," Rosa said.

"It's a shoulder bag," Suit said. "I bought it for the occasion."

"Sure," she said. "You won't be able to use the tape in court."

"Don't plan to," Jesse said. "I plan to see what she says, and then interview a guy in Boston and see what he says, and then, maybe, if what they say doesn't match . . ."

"You'll play each other's tapes for them."

Jesse nodded.

"You ready, Suit?"

"Yeah. I tested everything in the hotel room. I'll start it before we go in. Leave the bag unzipped. Tape'll run for ninety minutes."

"What's your first name?" Rosa said to Suit.

"Suit, short for Suitcase," he said. "I mean, that's not my real name. My real name is Luther, but there was a ballplayer named Suitcase Simpson . . ."

Rosa nodded.

"And it's a lot better than being Luther," she said.

"Well," Suit said, "maybe a little better."

Rosa was wearing black boots with a medium heel, black pants, a white shirt, and a yellow blazer. When they got to the front door of Lorrie Weeks's building, she reached into the pocket of her blazer and took out her badge. As they walked past the doorman, Jesse noticed that she shifted slightly into a cop swagger. He smiled to himself. He wondered if he did that. Because she was pretty and small, it was probably more noticeable.

At the reception desk, Jesse said, "Lorrie Weeks?"

The woman at the desk said, "Who may I say is calling?"

Rosa held up her badge.

"Detective Sanchez," Rosa said firmly, "New York City police."

The reception woman made the call and then took them up to Lorrie Weeks's apartment. In the elevator, Suit put his hand inside his shoulder bag and turned on the tape recorder. Lorrie's place was one of only two on the floor. She looked worried when she opened the door. But people often do, Jesse thought, when the cops come calling.

"Oh," she said when she saw Jesse. "It's you. What is it?"

"We need to talk," Jesse said. "You remember Officer Simpson. This is Detective Sanchez. Since we're in New York, she'll be the law in the room."

Lorrie stepped away from the door. The reception lady looked like she wanted to know more, realized no one was going to tell her more, and walked discreetly away back to the elevator. Jesse went into a vast living room with huge picture windows.

"What is it?" Lorrie said. "Is it anything bad?"

"No," Jesse said. "We just have some new information, and we wanted to see if you could help us interpret it."

"I'll be glad to try," she said.

"Good," Jesse said.

**55**

Rosa Sanchez stood in front of the big window wall and looked at the view. Suit sat in a green-and-gold brocade chair with his notebook, and Jesse sat at one end of a big green leather couch with Lorrie at the other. She was wearing a short summer dress, white with big red flowers on it, and when she crossed her legs she showed a lot of thigh.

*Good thigh.*

"Your maiden name was Lorrie Pilarcik," Jesse said.

"How did you know that?" Lorrie said.

"Advanced investigative techniques," Jesse said. "And you married Walton Weeks on August twenty-sixth, 1990. In Baltimore."

Lorrie nodded. Her eyes were open very wide, her lips slightly parted and glossy. She touched her bottom lip with the tip of her tongue.

"At the Harbor Court Hotel," Jesse said.

Lorrie nodded again.

"Yes," she said. "It was quite lovely."

Jesse smiled at her and nodded back.

"I'll bet it was," Jesse said. "Was it your first marriage?"

Lorrie blinked, her mouth still slightly open, the tip of her tongue moving back and forth on her lower lip.

"I beg your pardon?" Lorrie said.

"Was it your first marriage?" Jesse said.

Again silence and the nervous movement of her tongue. Jesse waited. Detective Sanchez continued to gaze out at the river view. Suit was quietly writing in his notebook.

"Second," Lorrie said.

"How long before?"

"Before?"

"How long before you married Walton Weeks did you divorce your first husband?"

"Oh God, I don't remember, a long time."

"You were granted a divorce," Jesse said, "in Las Vegas on August fifteenth, 1990, after six weeks of residency."

"Why are you doing this?" Lorrie said. "Why are you asking me these things and trying to trick me?"

"Trying to give you a chance to be honest," Jesse said. "What was your first husband's name?"

Lorrie stood suddenly and stood in front of Jesse with her hands on her hips and leaned slightly toward him.

"Conrad Lutz," she said. "Okay? Is that what you want to hear? I was married to Conrad Lutz."

Rosa Sanchez turned from the view and folded her arms and looked at Lorrie. Suit continued to make notes.

"Which is how you met Walton Weeks," Jesse said.

"So?"

"Tell me about that?" Jesse said.

"There's nothing to tell. Conrad and I were at the end of our relationship, and Walton and I were just beginning."

"Did they overlap?"

"It happens," Lorrie said.

"How did Conrad feel about it."

Lorrie said, "He knew we were done."

"So it wasn't Weeks that broke up the marriage?"

"No."

"What did?"

"Why do you care?" Lorrie said.

Jesse smiled.

"Advanced investigative technique," he said. "Just covering all the bases."

Lorrie nodded.

"So what broke up your first marriage?" Jesse said.

"Boredom, I suppose . . . and . . ." Lorrie stopped.

"And?"

"Well, I don't know how to say it without sounding terrible."

"We won't judge you," Jesse said.

"I . . . I don't come from circumstances as elegant as you might think," Lorrie said. "When I was a young woman, it was exciting to marry a policeman."

"At any age," Jesse said.

Across the room, Rosa Sanchez smiled.

"But then he went to work for Walton," Lorrie said. "And I started to move in a different world. And meet different people. And . . . it wasn't so exciting anymore to be married to a policeman."

"Or a bodyguard."

"Or a bodyguard," Lorrie said.

"And Lutz didn't mind?" Jesse said.

"Well, I suppose, of course, he must have minded," Lorrie said.

"And do you think he minded when you married Weeks?"

"Well, I guess," Lorrie said. "I suppose so."

"But he stayed on as Weeks's bodyguard."

"Yes."

"Why?"

"It was a good job," Lorrie said.

Jesse nodded.

"Do you think he might have minded enough to kill Weeks and hang him in a public park?" he said.

"Oh my God," Lorrie said.

Jesse waited. Lorrie's tongue flicked her lower lip.

"Oh my God," Lorrie said again.

"Whaddya think?" Jesse said.

"Well, I, my God . . . of course Conrad had some violence in him. A policeman. A bodyguard. He carried a gun. . . ."

"Maybe?" Jesse said.

"There was a lot of force in Conrad," Lorrie said. "A lot of passion."

"So you're saying he might have done it?"

"I suppose."

They were quiet.

After a moment Lorrie said, "It could have been Conrad."

"Any idea why he waited so long?" Jesse said.

Lorrie looked faintly startled.

"So long?" she said.

"You married Weeks in 1990," Jesse said.

"Conrad could be like that, very patient, very calculating, very cold."

"But forceful and passionate," Jesse said.

"Yes."

"And having been patient and calculating all this time," Jesse said, "have you any thought as to what might have caused him to act now?"

"I . . . maybe it was because Walton was going to fire him."

"You know that?"

"Walton mentioned to me that he was considering it."

"He say why?" Jesse asked.

"No. Just that he was thinking about it."

"Once he didn't have the good job," Jesse said, "there would be no reason not to kill Weeks."

"You know," Lorrie said. "That sort of makes sense."

"And the girl?"

"Maybe he had to because she saw him do it," Lorrie said.

"Good thought," Jesse said. "Have you seen much of him lately?"

"Not really, not since Walton died," Lorrie said.

Jesse nodded.

"Is there anything else you could tell us about all this?"

"It's just that I never thought of Conrad," she said.

"But now that you have?" Jesse said.

"I hate to even think it, but it makes a kind of sense."

"Yes," Jesse said. "It does."

56

How come you didn't tell her how we saw her with Lutz and Hendricks, taking turns?" Suit said as they were drinking coffee with Rosa Sanchez near the station house on West 10th.

"We can always ask her later," Jesse said. "I was sort of interested in how far she'd go with Lutz."

Suit took the tape recorder from his shoulder bag and put it on the table. He pressed play.

"*It's just that I never thought of Conrad,*" Lorrie said.

"*But now that you have?*" Jesse said.

"*I hate to even think it,*" Lorrie said, "*but it makes a kind of sense.*"

Suit pressed stop.

"Just making sure we got it?" he said.

"You're going to play selected portions for this Lutz fella?" Rosa said.

"Yes," Jesse said.

Suit nodded.

"And we got our pictures," Suit said.

"Worth a thousand words," Jesse said.

"You think this guy Lutz did your murders?" Rosa said.

"Maybe."

"You think the woman is involved with him?"

"Maybe."

"And you're going to use her to try and shake him loose," Rosa said.

"Yep."

"And him to shake her loose?" Rosa said.

"Yep."

"You think they're the ones?"

"She's been lying about absolutely everything since I started talking to her. He has never told me any of what you heard me talk with her about."

"We both know it doesn't mean they did it," Rosa said.

"And we both know it doesn't mean they didn't," Jesse said.

"That's right," Rosa said. "It's grounds for suspicion."

"She didn't mention that Weeks was divorcing her," Suit said.

"Her husband that's dead?" Rosa said. "The talk-show guy?"

"Yes," Jesse said.

"Was it going to be a good deal for her?" Rosa said.

"No."

"No money?"

"Not enough," Jesse said. "That was going to go to the woman who died with him, and their unborn son."

"Jesus Christ," Rosa said. "A motive."

"Sounds like one," Jesse said.

"But?"

"But I need to figure out where Lutz is in this," Jesse said. "I doubt that she could have done it alone. And why in hell would he do it for her?"

"He's been seeing her," Suit said.

"So has Hendricks," Jesse said.

"Who's Hendricks," Rosa said.

Jesse told her.

"He got something going with what'shername Lorrie?" Rosa said.

"So I'm told."

"And we got our pictures," Suit said.

"Suit did the photography," Jesse said. "He's very proud."

"A job worth doing . . ." Suit said.

"You think he's in?" Rosa said.

"Hendricks? Don't know. Can't rule him out."

Rosa took a card from her purse and gave it to Jesse. "You guys need me again, call. Deputy superintendent says I'm yours when you need me, unless something comes up."

"Thanks, Rosa," Jesse said.

"It was a pleasure watching you work in the interview, smooth, pleasant, keep her talking, show her a way to look good, and, if she's guilty, throw the blame someplace else," Rosa said. "You're pretty good."

"Thanks for noticing," Jesse said.

"She may have killed her husband and his girlfriend and their unborn child," Rosa said. "And she might have two male accomplices, and she might be bopping them both."

"And she looks like a charity-ball trophy wife," Jesse said.

"Appearances can be deceiving," Rosa said.

"But not forever," Jesse said.

**57**

Molly brought Lutz into Jesse's office. *He looks tired,* Jesse thought.

"Thanks for coming in," Jesse said.

Lutz nodded and sat down. Molly left.

"I'm not going to fuck around with this," Jesse said. "I think you're in a mess."

Lutz had no reaction.

"Here's what we know. We know you were a cop. We know you once busted Weeks for public indecency, and went on to become his bodyguard. We know you were once married to Lorraine Pilarcik, now known as Lorrie Weeks. We know you and she got a Vegas quickie divorce eleven days before she married Weeks. We know you seemed to have weathered this domestic upheaval and continued in Weeks's employ. We know you were just with her in New York, and continue to have a relationship with her, which gives the appearance, at least, of intimacy."

Lutz didn't speak. He sat straight in the chair. His arms crossed. His face blank.

"We know that Carey Longley was pregnant with Weeks's baby. We know that Weeks, prior to his death, had filed for divorce from Lorrie, which would have meant that all he owned would go to Carey and the unborn child, once the divorce happened."

Lutz didn't move. He looked at Jesse with the dead-eyed cop stare that Jesse himself had mastered so long ago. It was like they issued it with the badge. Even Molly could do it if required.

"We know you were a cop, so we assume you know how to shoot. We assume you had some knowledge of the degree to which storing a cadaver in a refrigerator would muck up the medical examiner's conclusions. We know you're a big, strong guy and could, if you had to, drag a dead body around and string it up on a tree in the park. And, as a former cop, you might have a better idea than some why doing so would confuse the murder investigation."

Jesse picked up his coffee cup, saw that it was empty, and stood to pour some more.

"You want coffee?" Jesse said to Lutz.

Lutz shook his head. Jesse put sugar in his coffee and some condensed milk and stirred it and brought it back to his desk.

"Care to discuss any of these issues?" Jesse said.

Lutz shook his head.

"Care to discuss the relationship with Lorrie Pilarcik?"

Lutz shook his head. Jesse shrugged. He took a tape recorder from his desk drawer, put it on his desk, and punched play. It was the tape Suit had made of the interview with Lorrie in New York.

*"And Lutz didn't mind?"* Jesse's voice.

*"Well, I suppose, of course, he must have minded."* Lorrie's voice.

*"And do you think he minded when you married Weeks?"*

"You recognize the voices," Jesse said.

Lutz made no answer.

*"Well, I guess."* Lorrie's voice. *"I suppose so."*

*"But he stayed on as Weeks's bodyguard."*

*"Yes."*

Lutz was perfectly still as he listened.

*"Do you think he might have minded enough to kill Weeks and hang him in a public park?"* Jesse's voice.

*"Oh my God . . . of course Conrad had some violence in him. A policeman. A bodyguard. He carried a gun. . . . It could have been Conrad."*

Jesse let the tape roll to the end, and stopped it and hit rewind. Lutz was impassive.

"She seems to think you murdered Weeks and his girlfriend."

Lutz didn't move.

"She was nice about it. She hesitated and lowered her eyes and licked her lower lip a lot, you know how she does, with the tip of her tongue. But very demurely and sweetly, pal, she fingered you for the murders."

Lutz moved slightly. Jesse couldn't tell if he was nodding his head or faintly rocking his whole upper body.

"Want to hear the tape again?" Jesse said.

Lutz shook his head. Jesse took a couple of eight-by-ten blowups of Hendricks and Lorrie that Suit had taken. He pushed them toward Lutz.

"You know the afternoons you spent with Lorrie recently in New York? She spent the nights with Alan Hendricks."

Lutz made no move toward the photographs, but Jesse knew Lutz could see them from where he sat. He stared blankly toward them. Then without a preamble he stood and turned and walked out of Jesse's office, and kept going.

Molly came in with a paper plate, on which there were two apple turnovers.

"You didn't want to hold him?" Molly said.

She put the paper plate in front of Jesse. Absently, Jesse picked up one of the turnovers.

"I got not one single piece of evidence that he has ever in his life committed a crime of any sort," Jesse said.

He took a bite of the turnover.

"His ex-wife says he could have done it," Molly said.

Jesse chewed and swallowed.

"Yum, yum," he said. "But she didn't say that he did do it. Any defense attorney in America would listen to that tape and see that I led her to it."

Jesse ate some more of the turnover.

"Plus," Molly said, "if it came to that, he could argue that she did it, and she could insist that he did it, and that would create reasonable doubt."

"So, no, I didn't hold him," Jesse said. "This is an excellent turnover. You get it at Daisy Dyke's?"

"I baked it," Molly said.

"Baked it?"

"Yeah, you know, peeled the apples and made the crust and added the cinnamon and put in the sugar and folded it up and put it in the oven."

"You know, turnovers are like donuts. They just seem to be. You don't think of anyone making them."

"I made them," Molly said.

"Wow," Jesse said. "Wife, mother, cop, baker."

"Department sex symbol," Molly said.

Jesse finished the turnover.

"Molly, I mean in no way to downgrade that, but you are the only woman in the department."

"So unless some of the guys are gay," Molly said.

Jesse nodded.

"Which I don't think they are," Molly said.

Jesse nodded again.

"Well, it may be a meaningless distinction," Molly said, "but it is a distinction, and I'm claiming it."

"Can I eat the other turnover?" Jesse said.

"Sure."

"Did you make them specifically for me?" Jesse said.

"No. I made them for my husband and children. But I saved two for you."

"Well, you're right, one takes the distinctions one can get," Jesse said.

"Besides, maybe a couple of the guys are secretly gay, and you actually are a department sex symbol."

"I'd prefer not to go there," Jesse said.

59

Jesse rang the bell at the front door of Timothy Lloyd's condo in the Prudential Center, and held up his badge in front of the peephole. After a minute the door opened.

"I'm Jesse Stone, the chief of police in Paradise. We need to talk."

"Paradise, Mass?"

"Yes, may I come in?"

"Yeah, sure, what's up?" Lloyd said and stepped away from the door. Jesse went in and closed the door behind him. He tucked the badge away in his shirt pocket.

"I am also Jenn Stone's former husband," he said.

Lloyd's face sagged a little, and Jesse hit him hard with a straight left. Lloyd took two steps back and then lunged at Jesse. Jesse hit him with a left hook and then a right hook, and Lloyd stumbled backward and sat on the floor.

"You can't come in here and do this," Lloyd said.

It always amazed Jesse what people said in extremis.

"Of course I can," Jesse said. "I just did. And I may do it every day unless we have a thoughtful and productive discussion."

Lloyd scooted on his butt backward away from Jesse and scrambled to his feet. Jesse could see his eyes shifting, looking for a weapon. Lloyd picked up a brass candleholder from the dining-room table, charged at Jesse, and tried to hit him with it. Jesse deflected Lloyd's swing with his left forearm, grabbed him by the hair, and ran him forward behind his own momentum into the wall headfirst. Lloyd let go of the candlestick holder and went to his knees and stayed there, trying to get his legs under him. He had more stuff in him than Jesse had expected. Jesse's business was to get rid of whatever stuff Lloyd had. He kicked him in the stomach and Lloyd yelped and fell flat on the floor and doubled up in pain and a kind of fetal concealment. Jesse walked to a red leather armchair near the front door and sat in it and said nothing. Lloyd stayed doubled up on the floor, groaning softly and occasionally.

Something annoying impinged faintly on Jesse's consciousness. He listened. There was a television on somewhere in the apartment. He couldn't hear what was being said. But he knew from the sound of it that it was blather.

After a time when the only sound in the place was the distant and indistinct blather, Lloyd stopped groaning on the floor.

"I never did anything to your wife," he said.

"You've been stalking her."

"I never—"

"I'm not here to debate," Jesse said.

He stood and walked over to where Lloyd lay on the ground, took his gun from his hip, and bent over and put the muzzle of the gun against the bridge of Lloyd's nose.

"If you stalk her again, or bother her in any way, or have anything at all to do with her, I'll kill you," he said.

"Jesus Christ, Stone." Lloyd's voice was up a full octave.

Jesse pressed the gun harder against Lloyd's forehead.

"You understand that?"

"Yes, Jesus Christ, yes. I promise I'll never go near her again. I promise."

Jesse stood motionless for a moment, the gun pressed against Lloyd. He could feel the air going in and out of his lungs. He could feel the latissimus dorsi bunch. He could almost feel it. It was as if he were able to project himself ahead into the sudden discharge of energy that came with a gunshot.

"Please," Lloyd said. "Please. I won't ever bother her again."

Jesse took in all the air his lungs would hold and let it out slowly, and straightened and put the gun back in its holster.

"Get up," he said. "Sit in a chair. Tell me your side of it."

Lloyd got painfully to his feet. Jesse made no attempt to help him. Half-bent and slow, Lloyd got himself to a big, barrel-backed chair and sank into it. They looked at each other.

"I don't want to make you mad," Lloyd said.

"Let's keep it simple," Jesse said. "You leave Jenn alone, you'll have no problem with me. You bother her again and I'll kill you."

Lloyd nodded slowly.

"Can I get a drink?" he said.

"Sure."

"You want one?" Lloyd said.

"No."

Lloyd went stiffly to the kitchen, filled a lowball glass with ice, poured a lot of Jack Daniel's over the ice, and brought it back. He sat and looked at Jesse and took a drink.

"I, you're sure you don't want something."

"I'm sure," Jesse said.

"I, ah, I liked Jenn a lot," Lloyd said.

The normalness of having bourbon on the rocks in his living room made Lloyd a little calmer. Pretty soon, Jesse knew, the whiskey would help as well. . . . *Coupla good old boys,* Jesse thought, *having a Jack on the rocks, talking about broads.*

"And I thought she liked me," Lloyd said. "But I think now that she just wanted me to get her into modeling, and television commercials, and, you know, help her career."

Jesse nodded.

"She was using me."

"Probably she wanted both," Jesse said.

"What do you mean?"

"Probably wanted to be in love with you and wanted you to help her, and she couldn't separate the two out either."

"I don't get it," Lloyd said.

"No," Jesse said. "You probably don't."

They sat on the seawall at the town beach in the early evening, looking out across the deserted beach at the empty ocean. Sunny looked great, he thought. Black sleeveless top, white jeans, big sunglasses. Jesse looked sideways at her. She was staring straight out to sea. He'd never been able to figure out what made a face look intelligent.

"You spoke to Tim Lloyd," Sunny said.

"Yes."

*Maybe it wasn't in the face. Maybe it was behind the face.*

"And?" Sunny said.

"He felt used," Jesse said. "He felt she was exploiting him to get ahead."

"I'm shocked," Sunny said, "shocked, I tell you."

Jesse nodded. He had stopped studying her face and was also looking at the ocean.

"He stalked her so he'd feel powerful," Sunny said.

"I know," Jesse said.

"To compensate for feeling so not powerful," Sunny said, "after she ditched him, or however he experienced it."

"I know."

They stared out at the ocean together. It was calm as evening arrived. The water moved gently and the surface of it was almost slick.

Jesse said, "He and I agreed that he'd stay away from Jenn."

"Does Jenn know?"

"Yes. But I'm not sure she's trusting the agreement."

"I'll stay on him," Sunny said, "for a while, see if he keeps his end of the bargain."

"He will," Jesse said.

"No harm making sure," Sunny said.

"Thank you," Jesse said.

"Did Jenn have anything else to say when you told her about the agreement?" Sunny said.

Jesse smiled at the blank ocean.

"She asked if we'd had a fight," he said.

Sunny shook her head slowly.

"That's so Jenn," Sunny said.

Jesse didn't say anything.

"What a thrill," Sunny said, "to have two men fighting over her."

Jesse was quiet.

"I know what you're like," Sunny said. "He wouldn't have had a chance for it to be a fight."

"He's an amateur," Jesse said.

"Sure," Sunny said. "And you're not. What's sad is that she doesn't know that, and she doesn't know what you're like."

"And you do," Jesse said.

"Yes," Sunny said. "I do."

Jesse nodded. He was motionless where he sat. He didn't look at Sunny. Nor she at him. They remained fixed on the slow ocean in front of them. A herring gull came in and landed in front of them, and snapped up a piece of empty crab shell. There was no sustenance in it, so the gull put it back and hopped down the beach looking for better. Jesse watched it.

"She knows," Jesse said.

"And doesn't care?" Sunny said.

"She cares," Jesse said.

Sunny continued to look out at the horizon.

"And she also doesn't know and doesn't care," Jesse said.

"We who are about to shrink salute you," Sunny said.

"I know her," Jesse said. "I don't understand her, but I know her. A while back, I thought we'd move back in together and it would be over. We'd be together. She wants that. I want that. And it didn't work."

"I like her better than I expected to," Sunny said.

"People do," Jesse said.

"She's everything you could want a person to be," Sunny said.

"Except when she isn't," Jesse said.

"Which is often," Sunny said.

"But not always," Jesse said.

A hundred yards down the beach, the herring gull gave up and flew away. The beach was empty now except for the two of them and the gentle, repetitive, heedless roll of the water.

"She have a shrink yet?" Sunny said. "I know she's had several. But I have a good one. If she'd go."

"She'll do what she'll do," Jesse said.

"And you'll do it with her," Sunny said.

Jesse didn't answer. The sun was down. It was still light, but the ocean had darkened. The wind had died entirely, as it often did at sunset.

"I think we need to say good-bye," Sunny said.

Jesse nodded silently.

"It doesn't mean I'll never see you," Sunny said. "It doesn't mean I won't help you. I don't know what it does mean, exactly."

She slipped off the seawall and stood in front of him.

"Except," she said, "right now it's time to say good-bye."

"Yes," Jesse said.

His voice was hoarse. He stood. They put their arms around each other. Neither spoke. Neither moved. They stayed where they were, hugging each other beside the nearly inanimate ocean as the twilight continued to fade.

J esse stood in the back of the room in the Town Hall auditorium while Molly held her daily press briefing.

"There is a development in the Walton Weeks murder,"
Molly said. "We have identified two suspects, and are pursuing several leads, though at this time we do not have sufficient
evidence to arrest anyone."

A television reporter in front said, "Can you give us names,
Moll?"

Molly smiled.

"Sure," she said, "how about Cain and Abel?"

"I mean names of suspects."

"Oh," Molly said. "No, I can't give you those names."

"Why not," someone yelled.

"Don't want to," Molly said.

"When do you expect an arrest?"

"Or arrests," Molly said. "As soon as we develop our leads more fully."

"Do you have a timetable?"

"Oh, absolutely," Molly said. "ASAP. Margie, you have a question?"

"I understand the governor has become actively involved in the case," a woman said.

"He has?" Molly said. "I'll be damned."

"You didn't know that?" Margie said.

"Nope," Molly said. "Had no idea."

"Is there a political overtone to this case," a man said.

"Here," Molly said, "in the Bay State? Hard to imagine."

"Are you saying the governor is involved and you don't know it?"

"I'm not saying what the governor's involved in," Molly answered. "I have no knowledge of any involvement by the governor in this case."

"Are you implying that his involvement is useless?"

"No."

"Useful?"

"What part of 'no knowledge' don't you understand, Jim?" Molly said.

"What's the governor's position on this case?"

"I don't know," Molly said.

"He's not made it clear?"

"I haven't spoken with the governor," Molly said.

"About this case?"

"About anything," Molly said. "I've never met him in my life."

"Has Chief Stone spoken with the governor?"

"Don't know," Molly said.

"Why doesn't Chief Stone ever meet with the press?"

"Doesn't seem to want to," Molly said.

"What about the public's right to know?"

"Chief Stone is mostly about protect and serve," Molly said.

"He doesn't care about the public's right to know?"

"Deeply," Molly said. "He cares about that every bit as deeply as you do, Murray. As we all do."

"Then why doesn't he talk with us?"

"He likes to have me do it," Molly answered. "He says I'm more fun. One more question?"

"What kinds of clues are you pursuing?"

"The ones we've got," Molly said. "Thank you all very much."

By the time Molly shoved her way through the reporters and got back to the station house, Jesse was there already.

"I saw you up back," Molly said. "Do I get a raise for not directing them to you?"

"Better than that," Jesse said. "You keep your job."

"I hope the two-suspects thing didn't get buried by the governor bullshit."

"There are enough reporters out there. A couple of them will recognize actual information," Jesse said.

"Think it will get anything moving?"

"I don't know. The tighter things feel," Jesse said, "the more likely something is to come squeezing out."

"As far as I can see, their best bet is to sit tight and do nothing."

"That's because you're not feeling squeezed," Jesse said.

"Except by the fucking press," Molly said.

"I thought Irish Catholic mothers of four didn't say *fucking.*"

Molly smiled.

"We generally don't," Molly said. "On the other hand, we're not ignorant of the phrase. There's the four kids."

"Worth remembering," Jesse said. "Lutz at least knows I know he did it. I don't know yet how much involvement she had."

"I'm guessing a lot," Molly said.

"Me too," Jesse said.

"So when they read about suspects and leads and stuff, they'll know we're talking about them."

"And maybe they won't be smart enough to sit still and do nothing. The whole crime has already been overthought," Jesse said.

"The refrigerator and the corpse display?" Molly said. "That sort of thing?"

"We both know," Jesse said, "when all is said and done, the ones you can't solve are the ones where somebody walks in, aces somebody, disposes of the murder weapon, and walks away. No motive. No witnesses. Nothing. This thing with Weeks and his girlfriend was badly overproduced."

"So they'll be inclined not to sit still," Molly said.

"It's why I think Lorrie's involved," Jesse said. "Lutz is an ex-cop. He should know better."

"What if he prevails this time," Molly said. "What if they do sit tight?"

"I know that one or both of them did it," Jesse said. "Sooner or later, I'll prove it."

Molly looked at Jesse for a long moment, then she reached up and rested her hand briefly on his cheek.

"Yes," she said. "You will, won't you."

**62**

As Jesse got out of his car in the parking lot, he could see someone sitting in the dark at the foot of his stairs. Jesse took his gun out and held it at his side.

"Stone?" the person said.

"Yes."

"Lutz," he said. "I need to talk."

"Okay."

They sat in Jesse's living room with the French doors open to the deck and the night air coming in thick with the smell of the harbor.

"You got a drink?" Lutz said.

"Scotch okay?"

"Sure, some ice."

Jesse got the whiskey and the ice and a glass and put them on the table.

"One glass?" Lutz said.

"I'll pass," Jesse said.

"I heard you were a boozer," Lutz said.

He put ice in his glass and poured whiskey over it.

"Sometimes I'm not," Jesse said.

He sat at the bar across from Lutz and put the gun on the bar top. If Lutz noticed, he didn't care. He looked past Jesse at the big picture behind the bar.

"Ozzie Smith," Lutz said.

Jesse nodded.

"The best," Lutz said.

Jesse nodded again.

"My old man used to say Pee Wee Reese was the best," Lutz said.

"Never saw him play."

Lutz shrugged. Once when Jenn had been staying there, she had put small-wattage bulbs in all the lights. More romantic, she said. Hated bright lights, she said. When she left again, Jesse never changed them. So the room was dim. Only the light over the table where Lutz sat was on. And it wasn't a bright light.

"Me either," Lutz said. "I only know what my old man said."

"He ever see Ozzie?"

Lutz shook his head.

"Died too soon," Lutz said. "You ever play?"

"Yes."

"Shortstop like Ozzie?"

"Shortstop," Jesse said. "But not like Ozzie."

"You any good?"

"I was."

"Good enough?" Lutz said.

"Got hurt," Jesse said. "Never got a chance to find out."

Lutz drank some whiskey.

"Tough," Lutz said.

Jesse waited. Lutz was quiet. He drank some more whiskey.

"Life's tough," Lutz said.

Jesse waited. Lutz poured himself some more whiskey.

"You ever been married?" Lutz said.

"Yes."

"But not now," Lutz said.

"No."

"She still around someplace?" Lutz said.

"Yes."

"Hard to cut it off," Lutz said.

Jesse nodded.

"You like this job?" Lutz said.

"Yes."

"I heard you was on the job in L.A. before this."

"Robbery Homicide," Jesse said.

"You got fired," Lutz said.

"Drunk on duty," Jesse said.

"Wife troubles?"

"Some."

Lutz drank some whiskey.

"They'll drive you right into the bottle, you let them," he said.

Jesse didn't answer. Lutz didn't expect him to. It was as if Jesse were barely there.

"So you ended up here," Lutz said. "And started over."

Jesse waited. Lutz drank.

"And starting over worked," Lutz said.

"So far," Jesse said. "Sort of."

Lutz shook his head.

"Too late," he said.

"For you?"

Lutz nodded. He was looking at his glass of whiskey. It looked good to him. He drank some.

"Bad mistake," he said. "Bringing it here."

Jesse was very still.

"Figured I had them up here anyway," Lutz said, "I dump them here, small town, some fucking hillbilly cop would be stepping on his own dick trying to figure out what to do."

Lutz added some ice to his glass, and some more whiskey.

"Drink enough, it doesn't do any good anymore," he said. "Doesn't change the way you feel anymore."

He drank again.

"Helps you talk, though," he said. "Instead of a hillbilly, I got you."

Jesse nodded.

"You seem to be the kind of cop I thought I was going to be," Lutz said.

He stopped and studied the surface of his whiskey again, as if there were something to be learned from it. Jesse waited. He was an exterior observer of a private unraveling, and he didn't want to intrude.

"But then I met her, and then I met Walton Weeks, and then I got really fucking smart. Or she did. He's the brass ring, she says. He doesn't want people to know you arrested him for public fucking. Make him hire you. And I say as what? And she says as a bodyguard. He's a big deal. He needs a bodyguard."

Lutz stopped talking and drank.

"So I'm his bodyguard," Lutz said. "And we're getting along. He's a pretty good guy, and I'm not demanding too much, and it sort of works, even though it shouldn't and I'm fucking blackmailing him, you know?"

The air got heavier as it cooled in the darkness and settled. The smell of the ocean thickened.

"Well, he's a cockhound, you know that. And after a while I think he's getting the munchies for Lorrie, and sure enough she tells me one day he made a move on her. And I'm saying I'll kick his ass, and she's saying wait a minute, don't be foolish. We can have the whole thing. And I say what whole thing and she says Walton Weeks, the money, the show, the whole thing. All she got to do is fuck him a little. And I say hey, and she says don't be a fool. I fuck him doesn't mean I don't love you. I'll be doing it for us, and we need to be a little creative here, and I can't say no to her, never could, and now I'm standing by and she's fucking Walton and then Walton wants her to leave me and marry him and she reminds me I gotta be creative, and it'll all be ours and we'll be together, but let's play this thing while it's paying off and . . . six weeks in Vegas and she gets to be Mrs. Walton Weeks, and I'm by myself stroking it, except now and then when he's not looking we get together. And she keeps reminding me it's all for us, and we're all that really matters, and in a while she'll get it all."

Lutz drank some whiskey.

"I used to be a tough guy," Lutz said.

He shook his head and looked slowly around the room, still shaking his head. On the low table where the phone sat was a picture of Jenn.

"That her?" he said.

"Yes."

"Good-looking," he said. "They're always good-looking."

"She's good-looking," Jesse said.

"And you're still hanging on," Lutz said.

"Yes."

"Why?"

"I love her," Jesse said.

Lutz gave a low, humorless whiskey laugh that sounded as much like a cough.

"There they got you," he said.

He nodded his head slowly.

"There they got you," he said. "So I hang around and she married Lutz and I stay on as his fucking bodyguard, sort of keep an eye on the investment, you know? And things are developing good until here comes Carey Longley, and Walton knocks her up and wants a divorce and everything is going to go to the kid. . . . The shit hits the fan."

"All that time and work and investment," Jesse said.

"She says I gotta kill them. And, fuck, you get the picture. I do what she says."

"You knew about the house in Paradise," Jesse said.

"Sure, I was there a few times. So that night, I brought them up to do a walk-through," Lutz said, "and talk about their plans, and where the kid's room would be, and when they got there I shot them outside, on the beach, at low tide, and let them bleed out, so when the tide came in it would wash away the blood. But I fucked up, I guess."

Jesse nodded.

"You found some blood in the cold room?"

Jesse nodded.

"Should have bled them longer," Lutz said.

"Yes."

"I don't care," Lutz said. "I'm not sure I really cared then. It was the last thing. Then it was over and we'd be together."

"And you kept them in the cold room to screw up the ME," Jesse said.

"Yep."

"And you hung him from a tree to confuse us."

Lutz nodded.

"Figured you'd be chasing wild geese all over the place," Lutz said.

He made the cough/laugh sound again.

"He was a public figure, you know," he said.

"And the girl in the Dumpster?"

"Another fuckup," Lutz said. "I wanted her to just go away. I covered her up, but some dump picker must have uncovered her and panicked and run off. Or sea gulls, maybe, or a dog . . . or maybe I was fucking up on purpose, you know? Like the shrinks say?"

He emptied his glass and stared at it and added some ice and poured more scotch.

"It ain't working," he said. "Scotch ain't working. Nothing's working."

Jesse nodded.

"And then . . ." Lutz said.

He drank and made his choking laugh sound.

"Just when you think it's safe to go back in the water . . . here comes Hendricks."

"And she needed to be with him to carry on the franchise and solidify your position."

"Yeah, yeah," Lutz said. "I didn't know we were both doing her the same day until you told me."

Jesse nodded. Lutz drank.

"So that's how it went," Lutz said. "She was the brains and the motivation. I was the patsy."

"And you killed a man and a woman and an unborn child."

"Yep."

"For her," Jesse said.

"I'm glad you get that," Lutz said.

"I get it," Jesse said.

"Maybe you're a patsy, too," Lutz said.

"Maybe," Jesse said. "But it won't help you. You killed three people."

"And you know what's pathetic?" Lutz said. "Everything I told you about her won't do you any good unless I say it in court, and I won't."

"You'll take the rap for her?" Jesse said.

Lutz nodded.

"So why'd you tell me," Jesse said.

Lutz shrugged.

"I needed somebody to know," Lutz said.

He finished his scotch and stood up.

"Now I'm walking," he said.

"You know I can't let you go," Jesse said.

"You got a gun," Lutz said.

"What is this," Jesse said, "suicide by cop?"

"I'm walking," Lutz said.

"I can stop you without the gun," Jesse said.

Lutz took a gun out from under his jacket and pointed it loosely at nothing.

"No," Lutz said, "you can't."

Jesse picked his own gun up off the bar top.

"I'll kill you if I have to," Jesse said.

"Close your case for you," Lutz said.

"I'll stay after Lorrie," Jesse said.

"Without me you got nothing," Lutz said. "There's no sign of her anywhere."

Lutz began to back toward the front door, the gun still in his hand.

"I don't want to do this, Lutz," Jesse said.

Lutz nodded and smiled at him sadly.

"But you will," Lutz said.

He raised the gun and aimed at Jesse and Jesse shot him in the middle of the mass, three times, his hand steady, his mind now empty, concentrating only on the shot. Lutz lurched a little. The gun fell from his hand. He went back another couple of steps and fell over, and lay on his side and bled to death on Jesse's rug.

Jesse stayed where he was by the bar and looked at the body on the floor. The sound that came after gunfire was always paralyzing. After a time he put the gun on the bar and got off the bar stool and walked over to Lutz and looked down. Lutz's face had lost all expression. His open eyes saw nothing.

"You goddamned fool," Jesse said.

Then he went to the phone and called the station.

63

Jesse sat alone on his deck, looking at the dark harbor and at the lights of Paradise Neck across the harbor. Lutz was gone. His rug had been cleaned. The press had left. The governor had called to congratulate him. Neat as a pin. He put his feet up on the railing and tilted his chair back slightly and rocked.

"Lorrie Pilarcik," he said aloud.

He could see the running lights of the harbormaster's boat moving among the moored boats in the near harbor, heading deviously for the town wharf. Behind him, through the open door of the deck, across the living room, he heard a key in the front-door lock. Only one person had the key. In a moment, it opened and then closed and he heard her footsteps.

"Jesse," she said. "It's Jenn."

He put his hand up and she took it and held it as she sat down on the chair beside him.

"You okay?" she said.

"I am," Jesse said.

"I heard about it on the news."

Jesse nodded.

"You want to talk about it?" Jenn said.

"Not very much," Jesse said.

"Have you been sleeping?" Jenn said.

"Not much," Jesse said.

"I remember what you're like," she said.

"I'm glad you remember," Jesse said.

"If you'll have me, I'd like to spend the night," Jenn said.

"That may not make me sleep," Jesse said.

Jenn smiled.

"I'm glad you remember," she said. "I'd like to stay if you'll have me."

"Yes," Jesse said.

"Would you like me to make you a drink?" Jenn said.

The night air felt clear in his lungs.

"Yes," he said.

Jenn went to the bar. Jesse watched the harbor boat wind toward shore. Jenn brought back scotch for Jesse and citron vodka for herself. They sat together and sipped their drinks and watched the harbor boat.

"I couldn't tell from the news why he did it," Jenn said.

"*Cherchez la femme,*" Jesse said.

"He did it for a woman?"

"He thought he did."

"Is she culpable?" Jenn said.

"I think so," Jesse said.

"Are you going to get her, too?"

"I'm going to try."

"But you might not be able to," Jenn said.

"Maybe not," Jesse said.

"Can you tell me about it?" Jenn said.

"Sure," Jesse said.

She listened silently as he told her what Lutz had told him.

"And you can't use any of what you know?"

"Not as evidence," Jesse said.

"The poor man," Jenn said.

"He killed two adults and an unborn baby," Jesse said.

"For her."

"He's the one who did it," Jesse said.

"And we're all responsible for what we do," Jenn said.

"If you don't believe that, what the hell else is there?"

"It's not always true," Jenn said. "We both know that."

"But we have to act as if it were true," Jesse said.

"So we have to pretend," Jenn said.

Jesse sipped his drink.

"I guess," Jesse said.

They were quiet. She held his hand. They were sitting so

close that her shoulder brushed his. He could feel her hair touch his cheek.

"You know," Jenn said. "There's something very odd about you and me."

"There's a lot odd about you and me, Jenn. We are a fucking mess."

"We are," she said. "A bad fucking mess. Me maybe more than you."

"There's enough to go around," Jesse said.

"But the odd thing," Jenn said, "is that in some weird way it sort of proves that love is real."

"It does?"

"We have every reason to be apart, and absolutely no reason to be together," Jenn said.

"I know."

"And here we are," Jenn said.

"For the moment," Jesse said.

"Why are we here?" Jenn said. "Together, after everything?"

Jesse tilted his head back and closed his eyes and breathed. His lungs seemed to have expanded since Jenn arrived. He seemed to breathe more deeply.

"I love you," he said. "And you love me."

"What else could it be?" Jenn said.

"Obsession?" Jesse said.

"Love," Jenn said. "Obsessive, dishonest, self-absorbed, whatever is wrong with it, and a lot is wrong, we love each other."

Jesse nodded.

"You know I love you," Jenn said.

"Yes," Jesse said. "I know you do."

"And I know you love me," Jenn said.

"Yes," Jesse said, "I do."

They were quiet for a while. The lights across the harbor on Paradise Neck were going out. The harbor boat was almost to shore. There was no sound except the movement of the water against the seawall below them. The only light on the deck was from the dim overhead in the living room behind them.

"We love each other and we can't make it work," Jenn said.

"Yet," Jesse said.

"What's wrong with us," Jenn said. "What is wrong with us?"

They sat quietly, watching the harbor boat's slow progress. Jesse shook his head. The harbor boat had bumped up against the float at the town wharf and turned its running lights off.

"A lot," he said, "and I don't know what it is, or how to fix it."

She nodded slowly with her head against his shoulder.

"But I guess we're in it together," Jesse said.

"Yes," she said. "I'm pretty sure we are."

Both their drinks sat half-finished on the table, diluting as the ice melted while they sat in the near darkness, holding hands and not talking, for a long time before they went to bed

2/0